'Tis the Season

by Alex Jane

To Rhys

Hope you enjoy!

Alex Jane.

'Tis the Season
Copyright © 2017 Alex Jane

Second Edition — 2017

Cover Design by Alex Jane
Edited by Alyson Pearce from Between the Lines Editing

All Rights Reserved

This literary work may not be reproduced or transmitted in any form or by any means, including electronic or photographic reproduction, in whole or in part, without express written permission.

This book is sold subject to the condition that it shall not, by way of trade or otherwise, be lent, resold, hired out, or otherwise circulated without the author's prior consent in any form of binding or cover other than that in which it is published and without a similar condition, including this condition, being imposed on the subsequent purchaser.

This book cannot be copied in any format, sold, or otherwise transferred from your computer to another through upload to a file sharing peer-to-peer program, for free or for a fee. Such action is illegal and in violation of Copyright Law.

All characters, events and places in this book are fictitious. Any resemblance to actual persons living or dead is strictly coincidental.

All trademarks are the property of their respective owners.

This is a fantasy world that only bears a passing resemblance to reality.

Thanks

Huge thanks to everyone who has been so encouraging and supportive as always but especially as I've been so nervous about this story. My immense gratitude to Milly, Cindy, Jay, Lillian and RJ for their invaluable feedback and beta skills, and to Masja and Alyson for wrangling my poor grasp of English grammar. And lastly, thank you to all my readers for taking a chance on this this story

For B.
Still miss you.

October

The wind whipped around the corner as Aaron stepped out onto the street—the music from the jukebox abruptly muffled as the door slammed shut behind him. He was whiskey-warm on the inside but the shocking blast of cold air against his exposed skin had him pulling the collar of his jacket up against the night.

It was cold for October. Cold enough that Aaron imagined he could feel the promise of snow in the breeze as it flowed down the street, casually blowing the golden leaves from the trees to scatter over the sidewalk, piling them in the corners of buildings or to catch in railings, before finally dying a water-sodden death in the gutter.

Realistically, the first snowfall was a long way off. It wasn't even November yet—not for a few more hours anyway—but still, the thought that the hard, dirty concrete glaring up at him would soon be blanketed safe beneath a soft layer of white made Aaron genuinely smile for the first time that day. Before long, he would be kicking through drifts of snow, not leaves; his boots crunching deep shoe prints in his wake, rather than leaving behind the flat, empty sound of his solitary steps hitting the naked sidewalk.

The thought of winter and all its implications sent a thrill of warmth through him. Or maybe that was the last shot of whiskey kicking in. The feeling lingered long enough that, even when Aaron's mind drifted to the fact John would have laughed at him for thinking such a thing, the memory didn't chill him immediately.

John had hated the snow. Or rather he made a show of hating it. He had bitched and moaned when the first flakes began to fall. But Aaron had often caught John smiling out of the corner of his eye when Aaron had stomped through a snow bank, or when Aaron had spent an hour making a village of mini snowmen to line the low wall of one of their flower borders, leaving his gloves sodden and face flushed from the cold. John's attitude toward winter had never softened but neither had his delight at seeing Aaron happy. At least, that was the way Aaron had always taken it. John stood steadfastly by his grumpy sentiment and rejoiced when the thaw began. For him, the spring had meant no more chains on his tires or driving around wrecks on the highway, or scraping frost from his windshield every morning.

Aaron paused for a moment, squeezing his eyes tightly shut against the memories. They never really stopped—flashes of a life that seemed more like a dream now—but their intrusions were getting fewer and farther between. He wasn't sure whether it was a good thing or not. His therapist seemed to think it was progress, but Aaron had lost faith in her after she'd suggested maybe he should at least think about the possibility of another relationship. He'd cut enough people out of his life for suggesting that very thing, or even that maybe what happened had been for the best and he should be getting over it by now. The memories were all he had left, and as torturous as they made his life, he wasn't ready to let go of them yet.

Cackling laughter caught his attention and he opened his eyes to see a rowdy herd of flapping, white specters racing down the other side of the street. One of them accidentally stood on the sheet of the ghost in front, causing his friend to be abruptly uncloaked. The shattered illusion—as much as it was—set the rest of the frat boys off into hysterical laughter while their compatriot tried to keep up and redress himself in the makeshift costume.

Aaron shook his head and turned away to make the journey home, an air of resignation in his step. A person could only wander the streets for so long, even on Halloween. But he dreaded returning to his empty apartment where he'd have no choice but to face his equally empty heart.

It was hardly dark, despite the late hour, given the seemingly endless parade of jack-o'-lanterns, glowing skeletons, and strings of lights in all manner of ghoulish shapes. Even without the festive lighting, East Harlem was lit up like someone was having a party all year round so Aaron always found some enjoyment walking back to his apartment late at night. It had been almost fifteen years since he had moved to the city but he still couldn't quite bring himself to think of the place as "home."

John had made the house they had shared a home, but now it was hard to think of the city that way without him. Yet Aaron had no reason to leave. Before he moved to his new apartment, he'd toyed with the idea of moving back to Duluth for all of five minutes before he realized he'd be an idiot. His sister still lived there but they'd never been close. Partly because of their age difference but mainly because Aaron's "lifestyle choices" had driven a wedge between him and his parents. They'd never gotten past it, and she'd taken their side. After their funerals, he and his sister kept in touch—birthday and Christmas cards, the odd postcard—but that was all. He never blamed her but he didn't miss her either.

Aaron was surprised to find himself humming a little as he crossed the pedestrian bridge back across the river to his apartment block; the song that had been playing in the bar as he was leaving. The bar was a dive but it was in a neighborhood his friends—the few that had stuck around, anyway—were unlikely to venture into so he didn't have to worry about bumping into any of them there. He'd stumbled across the place when he'd been at his worst, literally falling through the door at eleven in the morning. No one batted an eye if he showed up still steaming from the night before to sit sullenly in a dark corner for the bulk of the day.

Even after he'd cleaned himself up and returned to full-time employment, he'd drop by the bar for a drink in the evening, often staying late on the weekends with no classes to teach the next day. He got to play some pool, shoot the shit with the regulars, and flirt a little with the barman who had a wife and two kids but didn't seem to mind. No one gave him a sympathetic smile or lay a consoling pat on his shoulder. No one looked at him with concern or pity. No one told him things would get better, hang in there, or maybe it was time for him to start getting out and meeting people. He was welcomed but anonymous, which was just what he needed. His friends loved him, he knew it, but there was only so long he could take their platitudes and their growing frustration that he couldn't move on. There was a limit on sympathy, it seemed.

He was almost at the far end of the bridge, still humming, absorbed with trying to place the tune—it was reminding him of a commercial but he couldn't think which one. Soap, maybe?—when he saw a shape move in the shadows on the bridge. For a second, he thought he had imagined it as the few other people using the walkway didn't seem to notice, but then the movement came again.

Under normal circumstances, he would have walked on by—keeping his head down like anyone else who didn't want to get involved—but for some reason, he was struck with anxiety rather than fear. Taking a more brazen look, he could see the shape of a person, darker within the dark shadow. He was somewhat confused as there was fencing in place to stop people from getting too close to the edge, but the shape was on the other side, nestled into one of the concrete pillars where the heavy metal lines that stretched up to suspend the bridge were anchored to the walkway.

Aaron stepped forward cautiously, squinting into the darkness, satisfied it was a man sat on the edge not some demon or zombie; just a young guy hunched over, looking down at the water below, his hands gripping the lip of the parapet as his legs dangled over the edge. From what Aaron could see of the face beneath the raised hood of his sweatshirt, illuminated by the lights reflecting off the water, the guy looked eerily calm. The second-hand light made him look a little pale, but his mouth was set in a position of such quiet determination. When his weight seemed to shift forward, Aaron's heart leaped into his mouth. Panicking, he stumbled towards the rail of the bridge, digging into the pocket of his coat and did the first thing that popped into his head.

"Nuts!"

The shadow-shape jumped and pushed himself back from the edge to sit heavily on his tailbone with a sharp exhale of breath as Aaron lunged forward with his hand outstretched. The guy's head whipped around, causing his hood to fall away revealing a shock of auburn hair, and gray eyes that glared at Aaron. Aaron, who was standing there, one hand gripping the security fence while the other held out a crumpled packet of pecans.

For a moment, Aaron thought he saw a fleeting look of recognition in the man's eyes, but he figured it must have been a trick of the light when only disbelief and confusion remained on the man's scowling face. "What?"

Aaron jiggled the packet in his hand, making the nuts jump and rustle. "Would you like some nuts?" He swallowed hard, knowing full well he looked like an idiot or a crazy person. Or both. He would definitely blame the whiskey in the morning.

The guy tilted his head. He seemed more astonished that Aaron was speaking to him than at anything Aaron was actually saying. Looking Aaron up and down, he stated gruffly, "Are you fucking kidding me?"

Aaron's arm wavered in the air. As he brought his hand down, the motion stuttering and unsure, he sighed. Hastily rolling the packet up and stuffing it roughly into his pocket, he nodded, keeping his eyes on his task, muttering, "No. No, of course. Stupid idea. Sorry."

He expected to see anger on the man's face when he raised his head, but the man looked sympathetic, guilty even. Something about the softness in the guy's gray eyes shot a bolt of courage into Aaron. The eyes or that last whiskey, Aaron never could decide which. "There's a diner 'round the corner. I could do with a coffee. You wanna join me?"

The guy narrowed his eyes and leaned forward, asking in the most incredulous tone, "Who are you?"

"You can call me Clarence," Aaron said, feeling immediately foolish. He didn't mean to say it, the words just popped out, showing him up as the gigantic dork John had always accused him of being.

For a moment, Aaron thought maybe he should brace for a punch or attempt to break into a run, but then the guy's mouth slowly stretched out into a smile that seemed to take them both by surprise, and a short, shocked laugh escaped his lips. He shook his head, still half-laughing as he looked back out over the water. There was something painfully sad about him in that moment, his shape broken into pieces behind the fence. But when he sighed, all the tension that had been in his body seemed spent.

He took a deep breath, needing more than a moment to make his decision, then sighed again as he pulled one long leg after the other over the parapet. He shimmied along to a small gap in the fence partially hidden by some foliage, squeezed through and dropped down onto the pavement next to Aaron. "Well, *Clarence*, I can't really say no to that, now can I? Even though you're a little early."

The sad smile that flashed across the guy's face when Aaron got his first good look was really something. Something strangely familiar, actually. It made Aaron's breath catch in his throat for a second as the stranger brushed past him. Aaron was so stupefied by the moment, he ended up having to jog to catch up with the figure striding ahead.

The bizarreness of the circumstances didn't really hit Aaron until they were almost at the diner. Here he was, on the way to drink coffee with some guy he'd accosted in the street. The fact that it was Halloween didn't help matters much. They walked together in silence, a respectable distance apart, listening to the tinny jingle of mechanical skeleton laughter and occasional pumping bass from the parade of houses and stores they passed. It was late enough that the younger trick-or-treaters were safely tucked up in bed and only the older contingent, fueled by alcohol rather than candy, roamed the streets.

When they were almost run down by a bewildering crowd comprised of sexy nurses, unimaginative toga wearers, surprisingly convincing zombies, and what appeared to be the Easter Bunny, Aaron chanced a look over at his companion. And found himself looking straight into those gray eyes again. He could feel the flush of heat in his own cheeks as clearly as he caught the blush on the stranger next to him before they both swiftly looked back down at their feet.

Aaron hadn't given much conscious thought to the man's appearance until then but that look—the lingering interest in it—had him thinking about the way the guy's sweatpants moved, giving a tantalizing suggestion of what lay beneath, and the way his broad shoulders filled out the slim-fitting hoodie he was wearing. They were about the same height, and from what Aaron could tell, with only a slight difference in age. But other than that, the only thing Aaron could say for certain about him was that he walked a damn sight faster than Aaron was used to.

Luckily, the diner wasn't so far that either of them died of awkwardness before they reached the place. His companion graciously held the door open, allowing Aaron to feel the welcome wall of heat coming from the kitchen before he was even inside. It had to be close to midnight but the seating area was far from empty. Aaron headed for a booth near the back—away from the front door and the radio blasting suitably monster-themed tunes—unzipping the front of his jacket as he walked. He jerked it from his shoulders and found himself sitting sprawled out more than he would like on the slippery leatherette bench. The booze had been keeping him warm but now in the heat of the diner, a lightheaded fog set in and he realized for the first time just how buzzed he was. Not drunk but he definitely beyond making any major life decisions.

His companion didn't seem to mind much, though. He slid onto the seat opposite, his lips curling up slightly at the corners at Aaron's attempts to get his act together. Aaron wasn't so inebriated that he didn't notice the man hadn't taken off his hoodie. In fact, his hands stayed deep in its pockets as he curled in on himself. It made Aaron wonder just how long his new friend had been sitting out there in the cold and dark.

The waitress moseyed over, a smile on her face and a large nametag that read "Mandy" on her chest. She had skulls dangling from her ears and a pair of sparkly, red Devil's horns on her head. If Mandy was unhappy having to work the Halloween night shift, then she was doing a damn fine job of hiding it. "What can I get for you two gentlemen this evening?"

Aaron returned her beaming smile with one of his own. "Well, I don't know about…um, George here, but I'd like some coffee, black, and one of your excellent cheeseburgers."

She nodded and scribbled before turning to Aaron's companion. He twisted in his seat, straining to look over his shoulder at the counter, as he said, "Is that pumpkin pie?" The waitress nodded. "In that case, I'll take the same as my friend, *Clarence*, and a slice of pie too."

Mandy nodded at them both and shimmied off, humming the Monster Mash under her breath. Then the two of them were alone. And suddenly this whole thing seemed like a really bad idea.

Aaron cleared his throat and sat forward, rubbing at his eyes and willing his slightly-blurred vision to clear. He sighed and looked out the window, through the glaze of condensation forming in the corner of the pane. He thought—hoped—that the guy, *George*, might see his way clear to starting the conversation but all George did was shift in his seat and surreptitiously pull his hands from his pockets into his lap to rub them together. They were still looking awkwardly away from each other when a different waitress came by and poured them both a coffee from the large glass coffee pot.

Having something to distract them seemed to help. Aaron pulled his mug towards him, leaning over it and relishing the bitter scent that wafted up, feeling better—more sober—before a drop had even touched his lips.

"I wasn't going to jump."

The words came out of nowhere, and all Aaron could do was frown across the table, his jaw slack with indecision about how to respond.

George looked embarrassed underneath the superficial glaze of indifference he was trying to project, while seemingly putting all his concentration into pouring a near-fatal amount of sugar into his mug. "From the bridge. I wasn't going to—"

"I know." Aaron shrugged, not wanting to make it a big deal.

"I just needed somewhere to think. Somewhere quiet." George moved the spoon in his coffee diligently, stirring slowly, never once making contact with the sides.

Aaron shrugged again. "None of my business. Really."

"It's just the view from there is really something, y'know? It's not like you can see the whole city or anything but what you can see is..."

Aaron watched with interest, trying to gauge whether or not to believe him. Aaron had no experience with that kind of thing. At least, not from the outside. The man sitting opposite didn't seem down on his luck in any discernible way; his clothes were clean, his sneakers looked new, and he'd seen George check his wallet so Aaron knew he had money. He looked healthy enough, his pale skin clear, eyes sparkling—although Aaron knew that didn't mean a thing. He seemed sober. Just…sad. But, for the life of him, Aaron couldn't imagine the guy wanting to plunge to an icy, watery grave.

Yet, there was something about his story—it niggled in Aaron's mind. Something about it wasn't quite right. Like the echoing feeling of recognition that wouldn't quit. It bugged him. But he could not rationalize why.

"You got lots to think about?" It was a lame opener but Aaron figured it might work better than a flat out *I know you, and I know you're lying about something, buddy*.

His friend took a deep breath and sat back in his seat. "Oh, I'm sure you don't wanna hear about all that." Aaron recognized the tone. It was the one he used himself sometimes, after having to explain over and over things he really didn't want to think about.

Aaron held up his hands. "I got nowhere else to be."

George looked a little reluctant. He fidgeted, sitting back in his seat, then upright again. It seemed like he wasn't going to talk, but then started, "I guess you could say my life is in a state of flux right now." He glanced up at Aaron through his rust-tinted lashes, continuing when Aaron gestured for him to do so. "This month has been…hell, I don't even know where to start."

"The beginning?"

George huffed out a laugh. "Okay." He wiped his hand across his mouth. "My boyfriend of two years decided he'd rather date someone else so I had to move out."

"That's…shit. I'm sorry." Aaron didn't really know what to say. Mostly, he was a little surprised the guy would be so forthcoming about the whole boyfriend thing with a stranger. He wasn't in the closet himself, but he still didn't advertise his preferences around people he didn't know. It was surprising to hear someone speak so freely.

George smiled although his tone was bitter. "Oh, it gets better. I also lost my job."

Aaron's mouth wanted to drop open. "In the same month? Wow, that's…Christ."

George rubbed his temple with his fingers. "I guess that's what happens when you're dating your boss." He looked up again, his expression poised like he was expecting recrimination and almost seemed surprised to find there was none.

"Only if the guy is an asshole. Tell me you at least got severance? And somewhere to stay?"

George nodded. "I'm crashing at a friend's place, or at least I was…" His mind seemed to wander, only coming back to the moment when Aaron ducked his head and caught his eye. "His girlfriend came back home a day early. To surprise him. So, unless I want to spend the tonight watching them bang each other on every surface of his one room apartment, I need to find somewhere else to stay."

"Ah." Aaron screwed up his face. "Yeah, that doesn't sound like a fun way to spend the evening. At least, for you. I don't blame you for leaving."

"Didn't have much choice. We came back from the gym and she was laying naked on the couch. Apparently, she'd forgotten I'm staying there. Jerry bundled me straight back out the door with his hand over my eyes so I didn't even get the chance to grab my toothbrush."

Aaron snorted out a laugh, then tried to school his features back to something more sympathetic. "I'm sorry. No, I really am. You need someplace to stay?"

George shrugged and looked down at his coffee, unconsciously touching his pocket where his cell must have been. "I'm waiting to hear back from a couple of people. I think most of them are at some big party somewhere. I'd crash at my brother's but he's out of town. There's always a motel. If I can find one I can afford that doesn't have bedbugs."

Aaron almost offered then, the words right on the tip of his tongue, like asking a stranger back to his place was the most natural thing in the world. But instead…

"This is gonna sound weird but—do we know each other?" Aaron's mouth dried up as soon as the words left him. And from the way George raised his eyebrows, the question clearly hadn't come across in the way Aaron intended. "Oh god, no! I didn't mean that to sound like a line or..." He sighed heavily. "It's just you seem really familiar. I thought maybe we've met before."

George shifted in his seat and looked anywhere but at Aaron. Finally, he cleared his throat and shrugged. "I get that a lot. But no. I don't think we know each other."

Aaron nodded, a little embarrassed and unsure of what to say next. It was a relief when the waitress arrived and slid plates of food between them so they could settle down to eat.

"So. What about you?" George didn't look up, just picked up a bunch of skinny fries with his fingers, dipped them into the lake of ketchup on his plate and stuffed the ones he didn't drop into his mouth.

Aaron tried not to stare but the combination of fingers, open mouth, and stuffing was borderline pornographic. He was pretty sure the way those full lips wrapped around the fries—overlapping slightly onto George's fingers, so they dragged a little as he pulled back—wasn't intentional but it didn't stop a whimper escape his throat.

The guy wasn't exactly handsome, or even pretty like some of the crowd that used to frequent the club John used to insist they went to religiously twice a month. But there was something about his sharp features, the hint of red stubble on his jawline, and the supple way he moved, which seemed to light a fire in Aaron's belly; a fire that had been all but extinguished for what seemed like a long, long time. It was unexpected to say the least.

Thankfully, George took Aaron's pathetic squeak as a question, rather than the desperate, wanton noise of a man who hadn't had sex in over a year, and elaborated. "What are you doing wandering around, forcing strangers to eat cheeseburgers in the middle of the night? You don't look like a trick or treater?"

Aaron huffed out a laugh. "My sexy mailman costume might still fit. Might scar a few people, though. I think those days are probably over."

"No plans for tonight?" The question was innocent enough.

Aaron shrugged and lifted the top of his burger so he could rearrange the pickles. "Few drinks. Home to bed. Halloween's not really my thing."

George nodded in understanding. "Me neither. Now, Christmas? I'm all over that, but Halloween, not so much." His attempt to look casual failed horribly as he asked, "Your other half mind that you're out so late?" before biting into his burger with an innocent air of expectation.

The way Aaron's expression fell and he leaned back in his seat, dropping the burger bun back in place, probably said more than his mumbled, "I don't have one of those."

George chewed slowly and swallowed. "Sorry." He looked it too.

Aaron smiled sadly and picked at his fries. "Not your fault. But maybe we should talk about something else. I kinda feel like I should say *How about those Mets?* or something."

He huffed out a laugh as he said it but his companion's eyes lit up. "Oh, you can say it but just be prepared for me to talk stats at you for the foreseeable future. Though, I'm guessing you're not much of a sports fan?"

Aaron shrugged. "Not exactly. I played a little football in college, though track was more my thing." He frowned at the massive grin that was spreading across the face opposite him. "What?"

George lifted his coffee cup and took a sip, before saying through a smile, "I think we're gonna have lots to talk about."

They did. Talk, that is. The words came easy after that. Aaron talked about college, about going into teaching, about how he loved his job and the kids, and hated the subway. His companion talked about growing up in Queens, about still feeling like he didn't know what he wanted to do with his life, although he'd been thinking about taking some night classes to supplement his degree, and about how his mom still knitted him a Christmas sweater every year even though she lived in Florida with her second husband.

The conversation kept coming along with the coffee until Aaron realized they should probably head out; especially given the fact Mandy was looking over at them, having lost the smiling expression that had adorned her all night. George must have clocked her too, as he pulled out his cell for the tenth time to check his messages.

"Any luck?" Aaron asked as he pulled on his jacket.

George shook his head without looking up. "Nope."

Aaron slid to the edge of his seat. "Look. I live just across the bridge. You can stay with me if you want." He quickly qualified with, "I have a pullout. Or you can sleep in the tub with the door locked if it makes you feel better." He meant it to be lighthearted but George looked at him like he was considering it. The bed. Or maybe the tub.

In the end, all George said was an almost whispered, "Okay," and followed quietly behind Aaron when they stood and walked out of the diner.

It was only a couple of blocks after the bridge to Aaron's apartment but George must have apologized about twenty times during the short walk.

"Are you sure this is okay? I really don't want to put you out."

Aaron couldn't help but smile. "You're really gonna ask me that again?" George stood a respectable distance behind him, hands stuffed into the pockets of his

19

sweats, his arms pulling in to shield his body from the icy wind, and just shrugged as Aaron turned the key in the front door. Aaron smirked and shook his head. "Come on then."

The elevator was thankfully working, although it still smelled like something died in it even though Aaron had complained to the super twice that week. Both men tried not to be too obvious about taking in a lungful of slightly cleaner air when the doors creaked open at Aaron's floor and they stepped into the hall.

Aaron didn't feel at all nervous, not until he unlocked the door of the apartment and let it swing open. He'd been so focused on reassuring George he wasn't an ax murderer or sex maniac that he hadn't really thought about whether the stranger currently walking down the hall behind him might be one.

George followed Aaron in, then stood in the center of the living room and looked about, clearly trying hard to come up with something complimentary to say. "You just moved in?"

Aaron frowned and shucked his jacket from his shoulders to throw it onto one of the dining chairs. "No. You want a beer?"

George raised his eyebrows, but nodded. "Uh, sure."

Aaron turned away as George unzipped his hoodie, deciding he was probably better off not paying attention to what might lie beneath. He felt stupid that the guy was having such an effect on him. It was like being back in high school, crushing on his chemistry partner all over again. It wasn't like his libido had completely left after John but he kept his attentions on the safe option. Porn, not people. Because people meant relationships, and relationships…well he couldn't handle going through that again. Not that he was imagining wedding bells with this guy—he wasn't that crazy—but the fact Aaron was attracted to him, and could be around him without freezing up or running out…it was concerning. Though the booze in his system was probably helping quite a lot.

Aaron grabbed two bottles from the fridge and flipped off the tops with the bottle opener shaped like a leprechaun which was stuck to the side of the refrigerator with a magnet. It had been a housewarming gift from his sister. It could have been a nice gesture but at the time Aaron took it as a comment on the amount he'd been drinking.

Taking a deep breath, Aaron crossed the room to where George was standing at the window.

"That's a pretty nice view."

Aaron nodded and held out one bottle to him. "Almost makes the elevator ride worth it."

George took the beer. His fingers lingering a little too long and his gaze becoming a little too soft and searching for Aaron to interpret it wrong. Aaron jumped back, shocked at George's brazen interest, but almost immediately regretted it.

"I'm sorry." George stepped away. His expression shifted back to the sad and embarrassed one he'd worn at the bridge. "I didn't get a chance to shower at the gym. I probably stink."

Aaron's heart dropped. The last thing he wanted was to make the guy feel uncomfortable, but his clumsy reaction had done just that. "No. You don't. But...you're welcome to shower."

George shook his head and tried to wave the offer away. "Oh, no. That's okay—"

"No, really. You still look kinda cold. It'll warm you up. Let me just get you..." Aaron didn't bother finishing the sentence as he was already moving. It took a matter of seconds to find a pair of old sweats and a teeshirt which looked baggy enough that George wouldn't be too constricted. They were a similar size so Aaron felt confident about handing them over with a fresh fluffy towel. "Bathroom's first on the right. Do you want me to show you the—"

Aaron made a double-handed twisting motion that made George laugh. He placed his beer on the coffee table as he walked towards the bathroom, juggling the towel and clothes in the other hand. "No, no. I've showered before. I'm sure I'll work it out. Thank you."

"No. Of course." Aaron let his hands drop awkwardly to his sides, and shuffled his feet. He stood, watching the stranger disappear down the hall. As soon as he heard the snick of the lock, his hands shot up to cover his face, and he growled to himself, "What the hell are you doing?"

Taking a deep, calming breath, Aaron placed his hands on his hips and looked around the room. He could see why George thought he'd just moved in. It had been more than six months since he'd had to decant his life from the old house to the tiny apartment, but there were still a few unpacked boxes of books in the corner. Plus, the only furniture he had was the couch and coffee table, and the small table and chairs which acted as a breakfast bar and occasional office.

Apart from that, the walls were bare, with a stained and yellowing finish that screamed unloved. The surfaces were lacking any of the personal clutter that would make the place a home rather than a place where he came to eat and sleep. No photographs, no knick-knacks. He didn't even have any drapes. In fact, the only decoration was the stupid magnet on the fridge and a blanket folded over the arm of the couch.

Unless you counted the basket of laundry, piles of papers, or cups and plates and take-out boxes which seemed to have piled up in various places. Suddenly struck by the urge to not look like the slob he'd clearly become, Aaron started bustling around. He hurriedly scooped up the pile of essays that needed marking from the coffee table, juggling them into something resembling organization and dumped them next to his laptop on the dining table. It took more than one trip to the sink to collect up all the used crockery. He contemplated washing it up but didn't want to steal any of the hot water away from his guest and instead went around with a garbage bag collecting anything that could be thrown away.

After quickly straightening out his bedroom—which mostly consisted of hiding the basket full of clean laundry and putting all the dirty clothes strewn over the floor into the hamper—he pulled up his music library on his laptop, and set some light, and hopefully innocuous, folk guitar to play softly. He crossed the room to adjust the harsh overhead lighting but as soon as his hand touched the dimmer switch, softening the light in the room, a feeling of ridiculousness hit him hard.

Who was he kidding? He wasn't sure what had come over him. All this fuss for some guy he didn't even know? It was embarrassing. And worse, the poor man was only in his apartment out of desperation. He only needed a place to lay his head for a few hours. The idea that Aaron was trying to—what? Woo him?—seemed utterly stupid.

Aaron cussed himself under his breath, and snapped the lights back to full brightness. He was still cussing himself when he strode across the room and cut the music off mid-song, slamming the lid of his laptop harder than was necessary.

"You can keep that on, if you like."

Aaron spun around.

George's hair was wet, slicked back by his fingers, much darker but still discernibly red. Aaron had been right, the clothes he had supplied fit pretty well. George might have been bigger than him but Aaron had lost a lot of bulk over the last year. Still, the teeshirt was pulled taut across his chest and snugly encircled his biceps. George was barefoot, and held his once neatly folded clothes crumpled against his side with one hand.

Aaron felt the heat rise in cheeks, and feared he must be glowing. He shrugged and grimaced, and tried to get some words out, but he knew he'd been caught red-handed and couldn't figure out what to say. He figured *Sorry, I've been thinking about boning you since the diner* might seem a little creepy so instead he just walked over to the couch and picked up the beer he'd left there. "I understand if you don't want to stay."

George's face fell. "Do—do you want me to go?"

"No! No, I didn't mean…" Aaron hung his head and slumped down onto the couch, clutching the bottle in front of him like it could shield him from more embarrassment. "I didn't ask you back here for—It's just that…"

Slowly, George moved forward and sat down next to him. Not so close that they were touching but close enough. "If I thought for one minute that was the only reason you asked me to stay, I would have said no." Aaron felt like the weight of disappointment that came with those words might crush him, until George added gently, "But I kinda hoped it might be part of the reason."

Aaron looked up to find the gray eyes suddenly shy and unable to meet his. "Really?" He felt like an idiot at the raw disbelief in his voice, but all he got was a shrug in return.

"Well—yeah. I mean you're...I don't know. I just figured if two consenting adults are attracted to each other and want to spend the night together it shouldn't be a big deal." He almost managed to sound confident until Aaron let out a huff of surprise. George blushed. "Or not. I'm probably assuming too much. Please, just forget I said anything. I can go if you want."

Aaron couldn't do anything but stare in disbelief. That this attractive man could possibly be offering himself up to him seemed too good to be true. But then why shouldn't he be allowed something good in his life? This wasn't going to be a relationship. He could have companionship even if it was for just a few hours. The last effects of the whiskey might have lubricated his decision-making process but regardless, he found himself standing slowly, deliberately placing his beer bottle on the coffee table, his voice shaky and unsure when he said, "It's late. I'm going to bed." He tentatively held out his hand. "You coming?"

George looked up, startled, the flush in his cheeks making his eyes seem even paler. Without a word, he slipped his palm against Aaron's and followed him silently into the bedroom.

Aaron didn't look back. He shook off George's gentle grip when he got to the end of the bed and quickly

shucked his jeans and shirt before he had a chance to change his mind. When he turned finally, George was just staring, his lips parted and wet. Aaron instinctively drew his arms up to cover his chest, even though he was still wearing a teeshirt—he wasn't brave enough to face anyone bare-chested. He
wasn't much to look at anymore. Not that he'd ever been much of a gym bunny but the last twelve months had seen him lapse to not much more than a couch potato.

He cleared his throat to apologize, to tell George that they didn't have to go through with it, maybe it was a mistake after all, but George took a step forward, coming so close, Aaron could feel breath on his cheek when George asked, "Can I kiss you? I—I really want to kiss you."

Aaron thought he might burst out laughing, he felt almost hysterical at the formality of the request. No one had asked him that before. He managed to keep it together and nodded, saying awkwardly, "Um...okay?" He didn't have time to berate himself for sounding like an idiot—why in the hell did that come out like a question?— because George leaned in, pausing just before he made contact, then ever so gently pressed his lips against Aaron's.

The sensation went straight to Aaron's cock, which was the first surprising thing. The second was that Aaron couldn't ever remember being kissed like that before. When John had kissed him it had been a statement, an act of possession like everything else he did. But this—this felt more like a question. George was so gentle. Not soft, or weak, but Aaron could feel himself gradually opening up, acquiescing to the subtle increase of pressure; the way George stepped into his space; the way he wrapped his arms around Aaron's waist like he wanted to lift him; the way his tongue slid between Aaron's lips to explore his mouth, and left Aaron hungry and panting for more. George kissed Aaron with his whole body.

"You have no idea how long I've wanted to do that." George nuzzled into Aaron's neck, his words breathy and hot against Aaron's skin.

"Well, don't let me stop you from doing it again."

George chuckled, though Aaron started at his own wanton words. He shook his head. "God. I don't do this, y'know? I don't—"

"You want me to stop?" George's words were sincere but he didn't stop working his fingers under the hem of Aaron's teeshirt and dragging fingernails lightly across his skin.

Aaron groaned and shook his head rapidly in short, sharp movements. "Hell, no. I just...can we...lie down...? I just—"

This kiss was harder, more confident and Aaron was glad to reciprocate. It felt like a dance, a wet, delicious dance that tasted of beer and sheer delight. Aaron could feel George's smile against his lips as they moved together, with hungry,, happy kisses as Aaron led them towards the bed.

Aaron fell, sprawling back with a surprised "Oof" when he landed. George laughed, not at Aaron's clumsiness, but rather with him, as he pulled the teeshirt he was wearing over his head. His skin was pale, with a scattered wave of dark auburn hair that curled up from below the waistband of his sweatpants, all the way to his collarbones.

Aaron found himself reaching out without thinking, and drew the man down to lay on top of him. They made out for what seemed like forever but not long enough; the knee nestled between Aaron's legs gave him something to grind against, while George leaned judiciously on his elbows, making Aaron feel like he was being constantly touched and caressed.

It felt strange having a man's body against him again. And this man was so different to John; Aaron couldn't help but compare. Sex with John was a power struggle. Even simple foreplay felt like it was all or nothing; you won or you lost. It had been fun and passionate. This was too, but it couldn't have been more different. There was nothing combative about it. Aaron felt like he was losing himself, drunk on the connection they were making. The way George moved was elegant, flowing over him, undulating like water, the hard line of his cock cutting into Aaron's thigh with every pass. Aaron wanted to see it, taste it, wondered if it would be as sweet as the man's mouth.

When he felt fingers move to his waistband, hooking in and pushing his boxers down, Aaron didn't think to do anything but lift his hips to help the process along. As soon as he was freed, he grappled to find the waistband of the sweatpants George was wearing, unsure of what he wanted more; to feel George's hand around him or George's cock in his own hand.

In the end, he got both. They fumbled a little, unsure of what the other wanted but finding some agreement eventually when they started to groan and huff with pleasure. Aaron was surprised when he felt George shudder and his fist grow wet. Aaron thought for sure he would come first. He was so close; eyes shut tightly closed. He almost didn't realize his lover was pulling away from him until Aaron felt a hot, wet mouth wrap around the head of his cock. Aaron bucked up with a shout, and tried to pull back, but he came seconds later, unable to resist as George greedily swallowed him down.

Aaron thought George would roll away from him then but he didn't. Instead, his lover stretched up beside him, tucking his body in close, running his hand over Aaron's belly, through the hair that ran down between his legs, brushing his still erect nipples with his thumbs. He kissed Aaron's shoulder lightly. "I hope you didn't mind me...y'know." He glanced down at Aaron crotch.

Aaron laughed. "I think I made my feelings pretty clear on the matter."

George beamed so hard he got crinkles around his eyes. "Well, I feel like I could do better. Maybe...maybe you'll give me another chance?" He put his arm around

Aaron's waist and pulled him even closer, like Aaron might suddenly fly from his grasp.

Aaron smiled and kissed him. "I'd like that but you have to give me a minute."

George started to smile but somewhere along the line, it morphed into a roaring yawn.

They didn't say much after that. Aaron pulled his boxers back on, and his teeshirt off, using it to clear up the worst of the mess they made, then they crawled under the covers together.

Aaron hadn't thought about the possibility of sharing his bed with another man for quite a while. He always imagined it would feel like an intrusion, like an invasion of privacy. What he didn't imagine was happily falling asleep in the arms of a man he'd only met a matter of hours before, feeling safe and comfortable. And loved.

****

Aaron awoke with a start. His nightly dream too real, too vivid, for him to stand it. He stiffened, and might have screamed when he felt someone moving in the bed with him, had he not quickly remembered he wasn't alone. It was Halloween after all and ghosts had been weighing heavily on his mind all day. He felt suddenly uncomfortable about the man in his bed. A man whose name he still didn't know even though they'd shared something so intimate mere hours before.

A wave of guilt and shame crashed over Aaron and he quickly and quietly rolled out of bed. He made it to the bathroom without making a sound, locked the door and turned on the light. He took a leak, the sound of it loud in the quiet room, then washed the flaky residue off himself with a washcloth. He scrubbed at his skin, wishing he could take a shower without waking his guest. After the fourth time he splashed his face with water, staring at the droplets run down his blank face in the mirror, he told his reflection straight that he couldn't stay locked in there all night.

Aaron made it as far as the couch. He couldn't believe he'd done something so stupid, no matter how right it felt. Sick to his stomach, with fear and panic roiling inside him, one word kept bubbling up over and over. *Unfaithful. You've been unfaithful*.

Except that was ridiculous. How can you be a cheater when there's no one there for you to cheat on? And besides, he knew exactly what John would say. He would laugh right in Aaron's face—that huge bellowing laugh that shook Aaron's insides—and punch him in the shoulder. Tell him in no uncertain terms to stop being such an idiot. That he should get back in there and spread his pretty cheeks for the guy. That some dick might get him to lighten up a bit. Aaron could hear John's voice, clear as day, booming and rich. Even though all John could manage at the end, through the tubes and masks and morphine was a weakly whispered, "Don't be alone,

Ronny. Don't make me fucking haunt you. Find someone to take care of you. I don't want you to be alone."

Aaron fell back on the couch, his hands covering his face, determined not to cry. He had promised to do just that, hushing his husband with kisses and promises as he held his hand and bent awkwardly over his hospice bed. He didn't want to be a liar, but it was too soon. Ten months seemed far too soon. One day, he hoped he would find it in himself to move on but it still felt like he had lost John yesterday. Even though the man in his bed was beautiful and interesting and kind. Even though they had talked for hours and slept together and it was everything Aaron could have hoped for.

But he was tired and didn't want to think about that kind of decision. Hell, George, or whatever his name was, might regret the whole encounter come the cruel light of day. It would be best to sleep on it.

Yeah, sleep on it. Things will look much better in the morning.

"Okay, baby. If you say so." Aaron mumbled.

I do, darlin'. Let me hold you tight, and you just sleep. I love you, Ronny.

"Love you too, baby."

****

When Aaron opened his eyes, he wasn't sure what was more confusing; the fact sunlight was streaming in through his window, or that he was covered in a blanket. His head was telling him that he had one—or maybe two—too many drinks the previous night, and that falling asleep on the couch continued to be one of the worst things he could do to his body. He didn't attempt to sit up, just stretched carefully, testing to see which bits of him were going to spasm; rubbing his eyes and yawning, moving languidly, thinking about his lazy day to come.

The realization dawned on him he might have forgotten something really important, just as his eyes opened and fell on the note scribbled on a paper napkin that was propped against the bottle of beer he'd left on the coffee table the previous evening.

In his rush to get up, Aaron flung the blanket off himself. The tail end of it whipped around and clipped the beer bottle, sending it—and the note—flying on to the floor. Aaron lurched for it, missing and managing to crack his thigh against the corner of the table as he landed on the ground.

He yelled out, "Fuck!" as he scrabbled about on the carpet but managed to get the napkin before it was completely soaked through. He shook the beer off the note as he staggered to the dining table, then dug around in his over-stuffed briefcase for his glasses.

It seemed like his was never going to find them, when his fingers closed around their familiar shape and he pushed them onto his face with a shaking hand, leaving a wet smear of inky beer down his temple.

Clarence, Thank you for being my angel. You saved me in more ways than one. If you lik...

The remaining letters gradually lost all their definition as the beer disintegrated the thin paper, diluted the ink and the words lost their meaning, only leaving a tantalizing suggestion of an offer, a name, and a phone number.

Aaron slowly lowered himself into one of the chairs, not taking his eyes from the paper. He spread the remains out on the surface, then slowly removed his glasses and leaned back. There was a part of him that was relieved the decision had been taken out of his hands but mostly he just felt like crying. He'd missed his chance.

Instead, he sighed, balled up the wet wad of paper in his hands and let it fall. As it rolled off the table onto the floor, Aaron watched it go with a resigned, "Well. That's that then." He didn't move from his seat for a long while.

November

It wasn't easy trying to balance his cell between his ear and his shoulder. The lapel of his jacket just wasn't designed for such a thing and his scarf was getting in the way, but Aaron figured if he stopped to talk for even a moment, the sad selection of groceries on display would get even sadder. It was bad enough he'd left it so late to pick up any dinner that he'd had to wander around for almost an hour to find a store that hadn't shut.

By the time he considered that maybe he should just go home and see if any decent restaurants were delivering, he'd found a small place with the lights still on. Although given the scant selection on the shelves, he wondered if they'd just had a really good day, or if the place was going out of business. Then, just as he felt hope blooming, his phone had rung. He'd groaned audibly when he had seen the caller display and felt like groaning again now.

"I can come get you. I can drive down. It would take no time, and Sarah would love to see you."

Aaron had to huff out a laugh at that. He could imagine Sarah waving her arms, trying to signal to Brian with a look of fury on her face. "Will you stop? I'm fine." He rolled half a wrinkled sweet potato in his hand for a second before he realized it was rotten, quickly dropped it and wiped his hand on his scruffy jeans. "Besides I only have this weekend to get the painting done, and the baseboards alone are taking much longer than I thought."

The despairing sigh was clear enough in Aaron's ear. *"You know you're supposed to do them last, right?"*

Aaron rolled his eyes and threw a bag of wilting lettuce into the basket that was hanging over his arm. "Does it really matter? Actually, don't answer that. Doesn't change the fact I'm not coming, Brian."

Brian hadn't so much offered a place at his Thanksgiving table to Aaron as simply informed him he would be coming. He only seemed a little offended when Aaron declined, but they'd been friends long enough that he wasn't all that much surprised. Aaron had been gradually making an effort to reconnect with people, easing back into his old social scene but Brian knew not to push it. It helped that the friends who were left acknowledged Aaron wasn't the social animal he had previously appeared to be. That he just wasn't the same without John pushing him.

"You're at least going to get something decent to eat, though, right?"

"I'm trying," Aaron muttered as he walked away from the produce toward the refrigerators at the back.

"Something other than animal crackers?"

It was an award winning performance when Aaron managed to sound mildly offended, even as he looked at the contents of his basket. "God, Brian. What are you, my mother?"

"Having met your mother, I'd say I'm justifiably hurt by that comment."

Aaron smiled. It was almost funny looking back, but at the time, it was far from it. Brian had been Aaron's roommate in college and had the misfortune to be around the one and only time Aaron's parents had visited him. Aaron and Brian hadn't really known each other very well at that point—taking different classes and not really mixing in the same circles—but after Aaron's parents left, a shell-shocked Brian had sidled up to where Aaron was slumped with his head in his hands, sat next to him on the edge of his bed, put an arm around his shoulders and had held Aaron until he could breathe again. Or at least until Brian mumbled, "No homo," which set them both off laughing.

"Yeah, that was a bit harsh. But honestly, Bri, I'm good."

"Not moping."

Aaron shook his head and smiled, switching the phone to his other ear. "I believe the correct term is grieving, but no. Neither of those things are on the agenda. Just decorating, beer, I'll watch the game on TV, and have a BLT in the morning if there's any bacon left."

There were voices in the background, Brian and Sarah's kids, laughing and screaming as they stampeded by, and for a second Aaron felt like saying "Fuck it," throwing down his basket and telling Brian he'd changed his mind. But as he glanced over towards the exit, he saw a familiar set of gray eyes staring at him.

"Shit."

"No bacon?"

"No. Yes, I mean... Shit. I gotta go, Bri."

"You okay? You sound freaked out."

"I'm good. At least...no, I'm good. I promise. I'll call you tomorrow, okay?"

"Okay." Brian sounded suspicious but he didn't try to get Aaron to explain. All Aaron heard as he pulled the phone from his ear without saying goodbye, was, *"You better damn well call tomorrow!"*

Aaron's breath shuddered out of him as he shoved his cell back into his pocket, and he looked down at his feet trying to steady his nerves. Then really wished he hadn't. He hadn't registered just how much of a mess he looked when he'd left the apartment. He had quickly pulled on his scruffy old sneakers and his battered old quilted, plaid jacket, topped off with a ragged gray scarf to come out. The jeans he was wearing were splattered in paint where they weren't ripped and holey, and although he'd showered that morning, he hadn't shaved for a couple of days.

In contrast, the guy walking towards him looked good. Really good. The dark blue pea coat made his hair look even redder, and dark jeans hugged his thighs. Even his shoes were buffed and shining so much Aaron could see his own unattractiveness reflected in them.

"Clarence. It's good to see you." The guy, George, looked unsure, clutching the bottle of wine he was holding to his chest, but he sounded genuinely pleased to see Aaron.

Aaron swallowed. "You too. Really good."

"Really?" George blushed a little. "I wasn't sure if I should come over or if you wanted to forget the whole—"

"I fucked up," Aaron blurted out. George's face fell and he shifted uncomfortably, clearly misinterpreting what Aaron was trying to say. "No, I mean I fucked up. I wanted to call you but I'm a klutz and I accidentally poured beer on your note before I got a chance to... I even went back to the bridge a few times—I mean—" He sighed, grasping for composure. "I did really want to see you again." It was Aaron's turn to blush then and he looked back down at the tiled floor, wincing at his stupid mouth running off. *Smooth Aaron, really smooth.*

George didn't seem to mind. He smiled wide and his body seemed to relax. "Oh, that's...good." He shrugged and let out a sigh. "I just figured I'd been too pushy and then when I—" He paused and just smiled again. It was so light and bright, Aaron couldn't help thinking he could get used to seeing that smile on a regular basis.

They stood grinning at each other for a moment, taking in each other's expressions, until Aaron cleared his throat and asked, "You ready for Thanksgiving?"

George opened his arms to display himself. "Ready as I'll ever be. Just heading to my brother's place. You?"

Aaron mimicked his gesture. "Redecorating. Landlord gave me the go ahead so I figured I could get it done over the holiday."

George's eyebrows shot up. "You're kidding me?"

Aaron huffed out a laughed. "What? You don't like the color?" He pointed at a smear of paint on his thigh, attempting a game show hostess flourish.

"But what about—" George seemed to stop himself and have to bite his tongue. "Please tell me that's not your dinner." He glared at Aaron's basket. "'Cause lettuce, bologna and animal crackers does not a Thanksgiving dinner make."

Aaron laughed and felt his cheeks heat up a little. "Says you." He was preparing to use the same spiel he'd used to placate Brian until the guy interrupted his train of thought.

"Come with me. To dinner." George swallowed hard, and said a little less assertively, "You'll be doing me a favor."

Aaron took a deep breath and started to shake his head. "Oh, I don't know—"

"Please." George stepped forward and touched his arm. "Please." His voice was soft, breathy and pleading, and Aaron had to catch his breath. "One more won't make any difference to them. And besides, if I show up with a hot guy, my brother might find something else to get on my case about for once."

Aaron laughed, then shook his head. "I don't know. I'm not really dressed for it and—well, doesn't your brother mind—that you're gay?"

George grinned and before Aaron realized what was happening, the basket was being removed from his arm. "You look fine. And Kevin? Well, if he does, he's got a lot of nerve, being that he's married to a guy."

Aaron sighed, feeling powerless against the gentle hand pressed against his lower back, guiding him towards the checkout. "Okay." He let the vowels draw out, then added, "But I can't turn up empty handed."

George shoved the bottle of wine he'd been holding into Aaron's hands, and grabbed a six-pack of beers from a shelf as they passed it. "There you go. Totally full hands."

He grinned and kept steering Aaron until they got to the short line at the checkout. Aaron smirked and tilted his head. "You really weren't kidding about the pushy thing, were you?"

George winced and took a step back looking like Aaron was about to take a swing at him or something. "Sorry. I'm sorry, I'll try not to—"

Aaron barely had to think about it. "Hey. It's all right. I kinda like it." He smiled gently, relieved when George's expression softened and he stopped flinching. "And if I decide I don't, I'll let you know. Okay?"

"Deal." George tentatively held out his hand.

Aaron took it, happy to feel the strong warm palm against his. "Aaron."

The guy grinned. "Dylan."

The cashier pointedly cleared her throat and rolled her eyes. "Miranda. You guys wanna hurry it up? Some of us have places to be."

****

It only took a few moments for the door to open, revealing a tall man, with short dark hair and glasses that matched the shirt-tie-sweater vest look he was sporting. The sound of laughter and music poured from the apartment, along with a heady aroma of food that made Aaron's stomach audibly grumble.

"Joe. Hey." Joe didn't seem the slightest bit surprised to find Dylan wasn't standing there alone. "I hope you don't mind. I brought a friend."

Joe smiled and waved them inside enthusiastically. "No, of course not. I'm glad you did, actually. I think we have enough food to feed the block." He stuck his hand out for Aaron to shake ignoring the fact that Aaron had his jacket halfway down his arms and his scarf in one hand. "And if there's any justice in the world, I hope you're Clarence."

Aaron had half-reached out to meet Joe's hand but had to pause when he heard that. His mouth dropped open and he turned his head, eyebrows raised, at Dylan who was shaking off his coat and rolling his eyes, as he whined out, "Jesus, Joe."

Aaron huffed out a laugh and shook Joe's hand. "Actually, it's Aaron."

Joe shrugged. "My mistake. Good to have you here. Come on in. Dylan can introduce you to everyone. I'm still wrangling the turkey, I'm afraid. We should be eating in about twenty minutes, so there's plenty of time to get some drinks in you."

Aaron smoothed down the front of his messy sweater and tried to hide the frayed cuffs. "Yeah, I'm sorry, I'm not really dressed for—"

Joe slapped him on the shoulder and laughed. "Oh hell. Kevin's in his pajamas. We don't do formal. We're just glad to have you here." And with that he jogged off down the hall, towards the sound of conversation and music, leaving Aaron and Dylan alone.

Dylan smiled shyly and gestured after the retreating figure. "My brother-in-law." He turned and hooked his scarf on the peg holding his coat, which was already bulging with garments. "Told you it would be okay."

Aaron nodded, then said quietly. "You told him about me?"

Dylan took a slow step back and wiped his mouth over his hand. "Yeah. Well. Not everything. Obviously." It was hard not to think about the "everything," seeing Dylan in the tight-fitting blue shirt, open at the neck just enough to reveal the smattering of curls that swept up from his chest along his collar bones, and the way the shirt bunched into his narrow waistband. "I told them you helped me out. Joe has a tendency to read too much into things."

Aaron tried not to let the throwaway comment gut him, but it wasn't easy. The dismissal stuck in him like a knife. He knew he'd screwed up by not calling Dylan after leaving him to wake up alone, and even if Dylan forgave him for that, perhaps he didn't deserve a second chance. But still, hearing his indifference was hard to stomach.

It must have shown on Aaron's face, as Dylan stepped forward with a look of concern. "I just meant— he gets carried away and I figured you didn't want to see me again...I didn't want to get his hopes up. He's a romantic."

Aaron nodded but didn't look up. Not until he felt a tug on his sleeve. "Come on. Let me introduce you to everybody."

Aaron followed him down the hall past the kitchen, which was a mess; full of steam and flour, stacks of pans and disco music. Joe was in the middle of it, apparently serenading the turkey with the baster while an older woman wearing a bright yellow sari laughed hysterically in the corner, holding a dishcloth to her face.

Dylan passed by, only giving a slight smile, so Aaron took the scene to be not so unusual. The living room opened up at the end of the hall. The wide space was full of an eclectic collection of furniture and people. Dark, wooden furniture was offset by bright fabrics and every wall space, bookcase and surface was decorated with carvings, and paintings, and at first glance, a fair few fertility symbols too.

Surrounding the large TV, the couch and accompanying chairs that had been pulled in around it were piled with people. The occupants were transfixed by the football game, but clearly all rooting for opposing teams as there seemed to be some good-natured banter going on between them, as well as cheering and clinking of bottles. Several people stood around the room in pairs, or threes or more, talking and laughing. None of them paid the slightest bit of attention to the newcomers. Only a guy sitting in the corner of the room surrounded by children seemed to notice. He bent and whispered something low to the kids, and they scattered screaming and laughing, to race down the hall.

Aaron could see the family resemblance immediately. Kevin was taller than Dylan, leaner but with the same auburn hair and pale skin. He loped over, beer dangling from one hand, and swept Dylan into a fierce embrace. "There you are." He released his brother and ran his gaze over Aaron. "And you brought dessert."

It was said with such genuine humor that Aaron didn't feel the slightest bit offended and simply laughed. Dylan laughed too, but still slapped his brother on the chest, making him stumble back. "Hey, enough of that, you animal. This is Aaron."

Kevin held out his hand. "A Clarence by any other name?" Clearly, Dylan had done more than mention Aaron's appearance in passing by the look of recognition on Kevin's face.

Aaron smiled. "Nice to meet you."

Kevin opened his mouth to speak but Dylan interrupted him. "Don't say anything to Joe, Kev. You know how he gets."

Kevin mimed zipping his lips closed and throwing away the key, although there was something about the way he was looking at Aaron that made him feel slightly uncomfortable. Clearly, Kevin took his big brother duties pretty seriously.

Aaron smiled sheepishly. "I hope you don't mind me gatecrashing. Dylan kinda dragged me here."

"He was planning on bologna for dinner. I couldn't let him do it." Dylan smirked and Aaron couldn't help but smile back shyly.

Kevin clapped Aaron on the shoulder. "You're doing us all a favor. Joe loves to cook at the best of times but Thanksgiving tips him right over the edge. I should stop letting him watch all those cooking shows but..." He shrugged and looked not-so-secretly proud. "Anyway, let me introduce you."

Aaron had expected something a little more formal but when Kevin simply straightened up and yelled, "Dylan's here, everybody! And this is his friend, Aaron," he decided to just go with it. There was a disjointed cheer of hellos, and glasses raised, and Aaron found a bottle of beer being shoved into his hand before Kevin headed off to the kitchen, leaving Aaron and Dylan standing alone together in the middle of the room.

Aaron took a deep breath. "Well, this is..."

"Chaos?" Dylan smiled.

"I was going to say 'not what I was expecting,' but yeah. Chaos'll cover it."

Dylan nodded and started moving to the side of the room where a large dining table held snacks, chips and dip and vegetable sticks. "Kev tends to collect people. He likes a party. And Joe's the same. It's like this every year."

"So, not just family then?"

Dylan laughed and glanced around the room. "Only me. The burly guy and the skinny girl yelling at the TV are Joe's cousins but other than that," he pointed from person to person, "upstairs neighbor, work colleague, work colleague, no idea who that is, work colleague, downstairs neighbor, and a bunch of old college friends." He turned to Aaron and beamed. "And new friends."

Aaron shook his head. "You think you're so cute." Dylan bumped him with his shoulder. "So, what does Kevin do?"

Dylan popped a couple of kernels of popcorn into his mouth from the handful he'd scooped out of a giant bowl. "Well, he was a social worker. I guess he still is a social worker but he's moving departments or something right now. Joe's a math professor. Like crazy smart. He was nominated for a Field's Medal."

Aaron turned to him and blinked. "Joe. Who was singing to the turkey? Field's Medal?"

Dylan frowned. "I don't think the two things are mutually exclusive. Serenading poultry might even be a requirement for all I know, but yeah." He glanced over his shoulder. Aaron's eyes followed, and through the narrow view they had of the kitchen, he could see Joe laughing and struggling to get away as Kevin twirled him around. "They're made for each other."

Aaron had to look away. The sight of the two men coupled with that phrase reminded him too starkly of what he had lost. He almost blurted out, *People used to say John and I were made for each other*, but it wasn't the time or the place. Not least because he was genuinely happy to be standing there with Dylan at his side. He hadn't been kidding about going back to the bridge to look for him. Except it was more than a couple of times. More like hours every night for two weeks until Brian told him to stop or he was going to call Aaron's therapist. Or the cops. Or both.

Aaron kept his eyes on his feet and sighed, trying to will the unexpected grief away. It got a lot easier when

Dylan pressed his body tight against Aaron's side and whispered, "You okay?"

Aaron looked up, suddenly warmer. Finding his face so close to Dylan's, he was tempted to lean forward for a kiss but he just nodded. Dylan licked his lips, making it clear the same thought was on his mind, before clearing his throat. "You want me to introduce you to some people?"

Aaron smiled and tilted his head slightly forward, whispering, "I think that would be a good idea, don't you?"

Dylan laughed, put his arm around Aaron's waist. "Oh, I can think of lots of good ideas but I kinda want to eat first."

Any nerves Aaron might have felt about being thrust into this new social circle quickly evaporated. Kevin and Joe's circle of friends and neighbors were welcoming and clearly Dylan was no stranger to them. Everyone seemed especially pleased to find he had brought a friend, although no one else mentioned the elusive Clarence.

Barring only a slight delay—undoubtedly caused by dancing of some kind—the food arrived, laid out in a sumptuous fashion on the tables along with a stack of plates, allowing people to help themselves. There was all the usual fare—turkey, potatoes, green beans, sweet potatoes, mac and cheese, the serving dishes seemed to just keep coming—as well as some curried vegetables and rice dishes the neighbors had brought.

Aaron somehow found himself tasked with helping one of the little kids, a girl of probably five or six with long pigtails and dressed in a sweet pink sari, who held a plate bigger than her head precariously in her hands. He followed her strict instructions and filled it with something from almost every platter, as they were all apparently her "favorite." Her mom smiled gratefully over at him when they got to the end of the line as she tried to juggle a baby in her arms and load up her own plate.

Dylan had been right about it being informal. With no table as such, chairs had been placed around the edge of the room and everyone found a place to sit. A couple of small tables were set up for the kids, and some of the more flexible adults chose to sit on the floor. Aaron had started chatting to an older guy sitting to his left. Walter was a widower and although Aaron didn't bring up John, his expression must have conveyed something, since Walter didn't dwell on the subject and kept saying things like, "But you know how it is," like he knew Aaron absolutely did.

It turned out Walter's grandkids attended Aaron's school. Aaron did his best to hide his sigh of relief when it turned out they weren't in any of his classes, otherwise he suspected the night would have turned into a parent-teacher conference. Walter had just started to bitch to him, and a woman who had joined in their conversation, about the amount of homework his grandkids had to deal with and how teachers should just let the kids be kids once in a while, when Aaron's ear tuned into the conversation Dylan and Kevin were having on the other side of him.

"So, when are you going to start looking for a job?"

Dylan sighed. "I have a job."

Kevin shook his head, sounding irritated. "Bartending is fine as a stopgap, but it's hardly a career. It got you through college, sure, but you're twenty-seven, Dylan. You need to start putting some effort into finding something more permanent. You know, if you'd just take those last few classes you'd be qualified to apply for a job at a gym or get private clients if you wanted to go in that direction."

Aaron couldn't help lean over and whisper, "You're twenty-seven?" He was only half-joking. Dylan looked more like he was in his early twenties, although Aaron wasn't exactly shocked to find Dylan was only a few years younger than him.

Dylan frowned and whispered back, "Yeah. How old did you think I was?" Aaron shrugged and shoved a forkful of mashed potato into his mouth. Dylan narrowed his eyes at him. "How old are you?"

Aaron quickly swallowed, not finding the implication that funny. "Thirty-one." Dylan made a show of looking aghast, so Aaron bumped his shoulder, mumbling, "Oh, shut up."

Dylan started to reply but Kevin interrupted their whispered conversation. "I mean it, man. I know this new job is better than working at Havana, although anything is better than working for that asshole..."

Kevin kept talking but Aaron's ear got caught on that name. He couldn't quite breathe for a second, feeling like his head had been plunged underwater. All the sounds in the room, all the conversation and laughter and music seemed to quiet, muffled by his spiking blood pressure. He swallowed heavily and laid his fork on his plate, hoping his hand wouldn't shake and drop the whole thing on the floor. It wasn't only shock. Anger and embarrassment were making a show too.

He leaned into Dylan's side. "You—you worked at Havana?"

Dylan turned to look at him. He chewed slowly and nodded, seemingly understanding exactly what Aaron was asking him.

Aaron huffed out a breath and tilted his head. "You were a bartender at Havana." It wasn't a question. It was a statement, a realization. A memory.

Dylan swallowed and quietly, with a surprising amount of sadness in his voice, whispered, "Yeah." His head dropped for a second, then he went right back to defending his life choices from his brother's seemingly never-ending concerns.

Aaron sat back, trying to let it sink in. It made so much more sense now. The feeling of familiarity he had gotten from Dylan. The way Dylan had been so forthcoming about being gay to a stranger. Because Aaron wasn't a stranger. Dylan had known exactly who

Aaron was from the beginning. Maybe even from the bridge. And yet he didn't say a word.

And of course, that meant if Dylan had seen Aaron before—known him before—it followed he must have seen him with John.

John had loved that club. It was just his kind of place, full of music that was loud enough to dance to but still couldn't drown out his booming voice when he was holding court. He was the life and soul of the party. Even when they weren't actually partying. Any time of the day or night, just being around him was joyful. He made everyone feel like they were the most special person in the room. And Aaron got to tag along for the ride. It was a pleasure to watch him, dancing the night away, flirting with the new guys who thought they had a chance, keeping everyone entertained and included. John made everyone happy. And yet, from the first night they met, he'd also made sure everyone knew the only person who could ever make him truly happy was Aaron.

If Dylan had worked at Havana, then there was no way in hell he wouldn't have not known John, and by extension, Aaron too. And yet Dylan hadn't said anything to Aaron, not even a hint that they might have crossed paths. Aaron couldn't decide if it was kindness—a gentle suggestion that he was more than simply the husband of a dead man—or whether it was a flat out lie designed to get him into bed. He closed his eyes and prayed it was choice number one.

Without thinking, he got to his feet, simply nodding at Dylan's concerned, "You okay?" and headed out of the room towards the kitchen.

There was barely any space left on the countertop so Aaron carefully balanced his half-finished plate on an empty oven pan and selected a tumbler from one of the glass-fronted cupboards. He filled it with water from the faucet and was taking a long draft when Kevin came in and shut the door behind him.

Aaron swallowed and looked pointedly at the door. Kevin waved his concern away with a large flapping motion, betraying how much he'd had to drink far more clearly than his steady voice did. "Prying ears. I wanted to ask you something."

Aaron frowned and leaned back against the sink, folding his arms across his chest. "Okay?"

Kevin sighed, rubbing at his temple. "Look...damn, he'd kill me if he knew. I just...I wanted to know—"

"Oh god." Aaron huffed about a laugh. "Are you asking me what my intentions are towards your brother?"

To Aaron's surprise, Kevin looked almost stricken. "Yes! Yes, I am. Look, I know it's none of my business—"

"Damn right."

"But there are some things you need to know."

All the defensive crap Aaron had been ready to launch at Kevin dissipated. There was a concern on Kevin's face that Aaron couldn't take to be anything but genuine. He started to nod and found he couldn't stop until he said, "Okay. Tell me."

Kevin straightened up, blinking slightly at the bright light. "All right." He scrubbed his hands through his hair and sighed. "It's just that Dylan's been in a bad place for a while now. I don't know how much he's told you but the last two years we've all been begging him to get out of that relationship. That fucking guy was poison. He took advantage of Dylan, used him, then made Dylan feel like all the nastiness was all his fault. Then after it ended..." Aaron didn't really need Kevin to spell it out, he could see it in his expression, but Kevin kept going regardless. "He seemed to fall apart. I was worried about him there for a while."

"So, what happened?"

Kevin smiled. "You happened."

Aaron shook his head in disbelief. "Me?"

Kevin nodded. "I don't know what went on between the two of you but he just seemed to turn a corner. I think he was really disappointed when you didn't call him but I think experiencing the kindness you showed him really seemed to bolster him."

"Kindness?" Aaron couldn't quite get his mind around what he was hearing. Even though he'd pined more than a little over their one-night stand, he couldn't begin to fathom what sort of relationship Dylan might have been in that Aaron's simple act of human decency affected him so deeply.

Kevin dropped his arms and took a step towards Aaron. "Which is why I'm begging you, please, above everything, please be honest with him. It hurt my heart to see him so broken this last year. You seem like a decent guy. I'd rather you let him down gently now than break his heart all over again. Please."

Aaron was standing there with his mouth open, trying to think of something to say other than, *"I could never do that to him. Not ever,"* when the door of the kitchen swung open.

It was Joe, carrying a stack of plates. He tutted dramatically without taking his eyes off his cargo. "You intimidating our guest, Honey?"

Kevin smirked. "Well, it is tradition."

Joe rolled his eyes and pecked Kevin on the cheek. "Yeah, well, so is dessert, so help with that will you." He turned his narrowed eyes to Aaron. "You too. God, I can't believe Dylan didn't say anything about dating someone. We're going to have to have a long talk later about how the two of you met and—"

"Joe. Honey. Now you're being intimidating." Kevin smiled.

Joe smiled back, all teeth and snark. "Well, it *is* tradition."

Eventually between the three of them, and a couple of the kids pitching in, the pumpkin pie and apple pie and lemon tart, and what seemed like twelve flavors of ice-cream, and cake and cookies, made their way to the dining table and everyone descended like locusts despite the majority of them complaining how full they were mere moments before. And all the while, Aaron tried to figure out what it was he was feeling about Dylan and the night they had shared together, and whether the fact that Dylan hadn't been one hundred percent honest made any difference.

Once everyone was sufficiently loaded up and back in their seats, Kevin stood up, strangely authoritative in his bunny PJ pants, tapping his spoon against his bowl. "Feel free to eat but this is traditionally when we get to share our gratitude. I'll start." He cleared his throat with a flourish that elicited groans from some, giggles from others. "I'm thankful for my family," He gestured to Dylan. "For my blood," then to Joe, "For my love." Joe patted his behind, looking solemn, and Kevin laughed a little as he said with a sweeping gesture, "And for you all too, the family we make. Thank you for coming and making tonight so special."

There was a smattering of applause and pie-inhibited cheers, then everyone took a turn. Some people struggled and ended up saying something cheesy or lame, others were genuine and heartfelt. The kids were the best, seeing their little faces light up at being given an attentive adult audience.

By the time it came to Aaron's turn, he felt rather emotional and had to clear his throat. "Um. Well. It's been a difficult year... I wasn't expecting to be here right now..." He looked down at his lap, grimacing at his own verbal clumsiness, but then he felt Dylan take his hand

and seeing the gentle, encouraging smile on his face, he went on. "But mostly, I'm just really thankful for Kevin and his pajamas, for making me feel so welcome while simultaneously overdressed." There was a small ripple of laughter and Kevin gave him two thumbs up. Aaron smiled and shifted in his seat, and Dylan didn't even attempt to let go of his hand.

Dylan sighed and smiled and, glancing at Aaron, said, "A few weeks ago, I felt like I didn't have much to be thankful for but...I'm thankful for Clarence. And bologna." He grinned wickedly at Aaron. "And especially nuts."

A couple of people laughed, bemused at the cryptic message, while Aaron heard a few Oh's he took to mean that it wasn't just Kevin and Joe who had heard Dylan's Clarence story and were putting two and two together. Joe was frantically slapping Kevin's arm hissing out, "I knew it! Why didn't you say anything?" but everyone's attention was soon taken up with the remaining guests and their contributions.

The rest of the afternoon carried on into evening in much the same way, eating and talking. There were games and drinking, and the kids put on some sort of impromptu performance that would have made David Lynch proud of its surrealism. Dylan didn't stick to Aaron's side, but Aaron could feel gray eyes watching him from across the room whenever they were separated.

When it started to get late, Aaron checked his watch, although not as subtly as he thought.

"You got to be somewhere?" Dylan wandered over, holding out one of the beers he was carrying.

Aaron shrugged and shook his head. "I just don't want to leave it too late to get back across town."

Dylan pressed his lips together, like he was trying to hold back. It was clearly futile. He stepped in close and whispered, "Stay the night with me? I have—I have the place to myself tonight. It's two blocks away. It's not...I mean—"

"Okay." Aaron didn't even have to think about it. The thought of letting Dylan out of his sight again was kind of horrifying. He'd almost lost him once, he was determined not to do it again. At least, not until he could figure out what was actually going on between them.

Dylan smiled. "You wanna get out of here?"

Aaron frowned. "It's a bit early, don't you think? I don't want to seem rude."

"Kevin just went to find the Monopoly board."

"I'll get my coat."

****

By the time they left, after endless goodbyes and hugs and promises to call—and a stern, "Be here on time tomorrow," from Kevin— it was so late they didn't bother even trying to get a cab back to Dylan's place. They didn't talk on the way. It was cold so they pulled their scarves up around their mouths. At one point, Dylan took hold of Aaron's hand and stuffed it, along with his own, into the pocket of his coat. It was a gesture that warmed more than Aaron's fingers. He felt a little guilty he couldn't enjoy it more, given that the pockets weren't built for two and the stitching kind of cut into his wrist. But it made him feel safe, cared for, even if it was misguided on a practical level.

When they got to Dylan's building, he led Aaron inside, neither of them speaking until they were standing inside the apartment. The place was small but crammed with furniture and stuff. Lots of stuff. Aaron had a passing thought about asking if Dylan's friend was a hoarder. There were books piled up, clothes hanging from every available place that could support a hanger; boxes and papers even covered the couch. It wasn't dirty; there was just a lot of everything. A pair of battered old oriental screens divided off part of the room. The futon behind it, that was obviously Dylan's temporary home, was in its bed position with rumpled sheets and blankets, and magazines strewn across it.

"You wanna beer?" Dylan sounded nervous as he stripped off his coat.

Aaron looked about as he unwound the scarf from around his neck before settling his gaze on Dylan. "Actually, I'd like to know why you didn't tell me you recognized me from the club that night on the bridge." He figured there was no point in beating around the bush. They needed to talk and the sooner they had this whole thing straightened out the better.

Dylan stared straight at him, then nodded. "Yup. Definitely gonna need beer for this."

Aaron followed him when he tried to disappear toward the kitchenette. "Damn it, Dylan. Why didn't you say anything?"

Dylan closed the refrigerator door and leaned back against it, twisting the top off the bottle in his hand and throwing the cap clinking into the sink with a lazy flick of his wrist. "As I remember it, you asked me if we knew each other. Which we didn't." He sighed when Aaron raised his eyebrows. "So what if I recognized you from the club? You sure as hell didn't recognize me. You didn't even know I existed. I served you drinks twice a month for like a year and you still didn't recognize me." He took an angry swig from the bottle, making the foam well up over the top. "I mean, I'm not surprised. Not when you were with—" He caught himself, clearly pissed at himself for saying too much, and bit his lip.

Aaron took a step back and a sharp intake of breath. But then he shook his head and bitchily snipped out, "You can say his name, y'know. I won't fall into a dead faint."

Except Dylan didn't say anything, not for the longest moment. Not until Aaron was surprised to hear him whisper, "I had the biggest crush on you."

Aaron frowned in disbelief. "On me?"

Dylan nodded and took another drink. "At first, I just thought maybe I just wanted what you and—and John had." Aaron knew he'd given Dylan permission but still, he felt oddly emotional hearing his husband's name uttered on Dylan's lips. "You guys seemed so happy and looked so good together. But then I realized I was so damn envious of him every time he went near you. That he had you. And I didn't." He scrubbed a hand over his face. "Christ, I can't believe I'm saying this."

"Me neither." Aaron grinned, and thankfully it drew a huff of laughter out of Dylan. It didn't go very far in lightening the mood before Dylan's expression became serious again.

"I'm sorry if I...I don't know...pushed you or...took advantage—"

"What are you talking about?"

"I didn't know, you see. About John. I thought—" Dylan squeezed his eyes closed and took a deep breath. "In hindsight, it was stupid of me to think you guys would have broken up. But I didn't know that he'd..."

Emotion built in Aaron's chest. "You can say it."

Dylan shook his head. "I really am so sorry. He seemed like such a good guy."

Aaron nodded, letting his chin fall to his chest. Then standing upright, he reached out, drew the beer bottle from Dylan's hand and leaned back against the kitchen counter. He took a long drink. "Yeah. Yeah, he was."

Dylan watched him, his face schooled in an expression of concern rather than sympathy, like he was trying to figure out a puzzle. Then he smiled slightly. "Was he always such a flirt?"

Aaron laughed. "Oh yeah. Even in college. I've no idea where he got the energy."

"He always managed to make us laugh, no matter what kind of shitty night we were having."

Aaron smiled and tilted his head. "That's my John." Except it wasn't his John anymore. His face fell, tears stinging his eyes and he scowled at the bottle in his hands.

Dylan stepped up, laying a gentle hand on Aaron's forearm. "I am sorry."

Aaron squeezed his eyes tight against the emotion that was threatening to spill out of him and leaned forward to rest his head against Dylan's shoulder. "Sometimes I think I'm fine, then it just blindsides me and I feel like I'm still in shock or something. It all happened so quick. One minute he was healthy as a horse, so full of life. The next minute the doctors are telling him to get his affairs in order and recommending hospices." Dylan's arms came up, pulling tight across his back. Normally, Aaron would shrug off any attempts at comfort from friends but this felt different. Like Dylan was there for him alone, not trying to deal with his own grief. "I miss him so much. This is supposed to be the worst of it—the first year. The first birthdays, first Valentine's, first anniversary...without him. First Halloween—"

"First Thanksgiving." Dylan's voice was rough with emotion. "Shit. Did I do the wrong thing? Inviting you?"

Aaron huffed out a laugh and pulled back to stand upright. "I think strong-arming me would be more accurate." Dylan blushed and looked away but Aaron cupped his cheek, rubbing his thumb gently across the blaze of stubble. "I'm glad you did. I really wanted to see you again."

Aaron leaned forward and kissed him. Gentle and chaste. Not much more than pressing their lips together but he felt a sense of relief, like he'd been holding some tension inside him that he could finally let go of.

They held each other for a long time, like lost children who had finally found each other in the darkness, eventually parting when Aaron tried to stifle a yawn.

Dylan sighed and pressed his body close as Aaron looked up at him. "What do you want to do?"

Aaron smiled. "What? Right now or on a more general level?"

"Either. Both."

"Well, right now, I'd like to sleep. I'm tired."

Dylan nodded. "And longer term?"

Aaron shook his head and sighed. "Honestly? I don't know. I feel like I—I want to be with you but—I don't know whether that would be the best thing for either of us right now." Dylan frowned and started to pull away but Aaron held fast. "I just don't know if I'm ready."

Dylan kept up the pressure until Aaron had no choice but to release him. But he didn't storm away like Aaron was expecting. He just took a step back, folding his arms across his chest, and nodded. "I get it, I do. I guess..." He sighed heavily and hung his head.

Aaron couldn't help but smile and tease. "So much for you being pushy."

Dylan looked up, shocked until he caught the smirk on Aaron's lips and echoed it back to him. "Hey, I'm respecting your boundaries, dammit." His lips pressed together for a second then he stepped forward again, leaning his arms on the kitchen counter, bracketing Aaron between them. "I want to see you again. I don't care if we just hang out and watch TV or whatever, but I do want to see you again. No pressure. For anything. Just friends."

Aaron smiled and hooked his finger into the open vee of Dylan's shirt, tugging on it lightly. "No pressure, I can do. Just friends."

Dylan smiled if a little sadly. He stood back. "Let me just fix the pull out for you. Jerry won't mind if I crash in his bed for one night."

He turned to leave but Aaron grabbed him by the wrist. "No. I—I mean, I'd like to..."

Dylan sighed, almost laughing but it sounded more like exasperation. "You're killing me here. My head's spinning from these mixed messages."

Aaron shrugged and tried to look apologetic. "Does it bother you?"

Dylan shook his head and looked away, but he was smiling. He pointed towards the door on the right.

"Bathroom's there. Should be a spare toothbrush on the top shelf."

Aaron found the toothbrush amongst half-empty bottles of mouthwash, antiseptic cream, eye drops and condoms. By the time he was done, Dylan had dumped his collection of magazines somewhere and made the bed. Aaron stripped down to his boxers and teeshirt and slipped under the covers while Dylan took his turn in the bathroom.

Dylan emerged already undressed, just in his underwear and a loose teeshirt. Aaron had wondered if he should pretend to be asleep already but he couldn't help taking a good look before Dylan flicked off the light.

Aaron held his breath as Dylan lay down beside him, trying not to think about how much he wanted to reach out and touch. He had meant what he said; it was unfair on both of them to get Dylan's hopes up. They lay still, flat on their backs. Aaron started to drift but Dylan cussed under his breath. "This is ridiculous. Big spoon or little spoon?"

Aaron turned his head on the pillow to look at Dylan's silhouette in the dark and frowned. "What?"

Dylan turned to face him and sighed, although he sounded kind of nervous. "It's not that difficult Aaron. Big spoon or—"

"Little spoon. I—I like to be little spoon."

"Okay then." Dylan went quiet. "Well, go on."

Aaron's sleep-stupid brain finally got with the program and he turned over, facing away from Dylan. Dylan immediately scooted up behind him and snuggled close. After a minute, he whispered, "This okay?"

Aaron nodded. Because it was. It felt surprisingly good and he let himself relax back into the space that seemed to fit him perfectly. Dylan seemed to feel it too and sighed out heavily, stretching against the length of Aaron.

As sleep started to take Aaron down, Dylan whispered again. "I'm so glad I found you again, Clarence."

But all Aaron heard was *Don't be alone, Ronny. I don't want you to be alone*.

December

Aaron sprawled out in one of Brian's huge puffy armchairs, illuminated by the colored twinkling lights on the huge Blue Spruce Sarah had insisted on stuffing into the corner of the TV room. It had taken Aaron and Brian forty minutes to get the monstrous thing off the roof-rack and into the house. To be fair, it had looked spectacular once Sarah and the kids had finished decorating it but the thing was already dying. And what with the cat taking up residence, rustling around in there and making the needles drop at an alarming rate, Aaron wondered if it was really worth it. Still, there was only one day to go, officially, and then Christmas would be over.

He was reaching out to the bowl of popcorn that sat on the small table nestled between his recliner and the one next to him, when his cell beeped. Aaron didn't take his eyes from the game. The quarterback was making the mother of all Hail Mary passes at the end of the third quarter. Anything else could wait. Brian, who sat in the chair next to him in a similar sluggish fashion, didn't look away from the screen either, just turned his head slightly towards Aaron. "You gonna get that?" Aaron shrugged. Brian snorted and rocked his head back to center, mumbling, "You're ridiculous."

"Your mother is."

"Well, that's true." Brian took a swig from his beer. "You should still answer him."

Aaron grunted but smiled a little too. A small secret thing that had started appearing on his face unbidden and with increasing frequency.

The receiver fumbled. Brian sighed, then caught sight of the look on Aaron's face and snorted again. "Like I said. Ridiculous."

Aaron flipped him the finger, more resolved than ever not to look at the message. He knew it was from Dylan. He had a hundred more just like it, and those were just the ones he'd decided not to delete.

Waking up with Dylan the morning after Thanksgiving was less surreal than it should have been. They had lain together and talked over what they had decided the night before, that they should wait, get to know each other, not rush into anything, until Aaron felt confident he was ready for another relationship. He'd told Dylan about his mixed feelings after their first night together, about his guilt and grief, and Dylan was extremely understanding and supportive. It was an adult, rational discussion. Which, of course, ended with Dylan fucking Aaron through the mattress of his futon.

Aaron started it. All he'd done was brush a strand of Dylan's hair back behind his ear, but that opened the way to touching, and then kissing. Before he knew what he was doing, Aaron was pulling Dylan's teeshirt over his head and tasting his pale skin anyway he could. He'd put the actual fucking part down to Dylan though. If he hadn't asked Aaron what he wanted while his hand was on Aaron's cock, then Aaron wouldn't have begged, "Oh god, I want you in me." Dylan obliged, first with his fingers then, after a record-breaking sprint to the bathroom and back, with his cock, which he delivered in a more than satisfactory manner. They didn't come together but it hardly mattered afterward when they had lain in each other's arms relishing the afterglow.

What had mattered was that Dylan had been concerned for Aaron. If Aaron was all right; if Dylan had gone too far; if he should have stopped despite Aaron's urging in the heat of the moment. For the first time, Aaron realized that was something he had been missing, and found himself acknowledging that he trusted Dylan; with his body, and maybe with his heart.

The only downside to the whole event had been that Dylan was leaving to go visit his mother in Florida. He and Kevin were flying down and would be gone until the New Year. Dylan had promised to text Aaron every day, twice a day, which he had. The first one came as

Aaron stepped out into the chilly November morning closing the door to Dylan's place behind him.

I should have kissed u goodbye

Aaron had smiled the whole way home.

When Aaron's cell beeped a second time, Brian threw a handful of popcorn at him. "Jesus Christ, answer it! Doesn't the man know there's game on?"

Aaron growled at him and lifted his ass cheek so he could slide his phone out of his back pocket, making the stray kernels roll onto the floor.

Telling Brian about seeing Dylan again hadn't been a big deal. Aaron had already been through a halting, anxious confession about meeting his mystery man at Halloween and Brian had been so pleased and relieved that Aaron was even considering seeing someone new, it made Aaron doubly sad at losing Dylan's number. So when Aaron had told Brian that he'd bumped into Dylan at the store, Brian just threw his hands up and announced, "Well, that settles it! It's fate. You have to date him now!" And that seemed to be the end of the discussion.

But Aaron had cornered Sarah one night after dinner while Brian was putting the kids to bed and asked her if she thought Brian was right. She wiped her hands on the dishcloth she was holding, looking thoughtful. "I think he trusts you to know when you're ready. But honestly? I also think he still feels immensely guilty about John, and the sooner you're happy, the sooner he can stop feeling so bad about putting you through this."

Sarah wasn't a hugger, but Aaron had hugged her anyway. And she didn't complain for once, just awkwardly patted his back.

Still, once the text messages started coming, Brian hadn't missed an opportunity to roll his eyes, or yawn, or flutter his eyelids and make heart shapes in the air. It wasn't so much an annoyance as a relief to have something fun between them that didn't remind them of the year they'd both endured.

This was no different. As soon as Aaron lifted his phone up and swiped the screen, Brian started making heartbeat noises and fluttering his hand under his sweater. He stopped pretty quickly when he saw the look on Aaron's face. "Shit. What is it?"

Aaron shook his head. "I'm not sure yet."

The message read, *How do u feel about surprises?*

Aaron's thumbs flew over the keypad. *Depends on the surprise.*

He quickly turned off the screen and balanced it on the arm of the chair, ignoring the fact that Brian was staring at him. It seemed like forever before the phone beeped again.

Well, if u come down to Alonzos at 7pm u can tell me all about which surprises u do like :)

Aaron's heart did a little skip and he couldn't help but take a sharp of breath. The thought that Dylan was back in town and wanted to see him set off a burst of happiness inside him. But there was something else, a sense of dread that stopped it in its tracks.

"So? What did he say?" Brian frowned across the chasm between the chairs.

Aaron cleared his throat and sat up a little. "Dylan's back in New York. Wants to meet me for dinner."

Brian shrugged and looked back to the game. "What time?"

"Seven."

Brian looked at his watch. "Cool. I can drop you at your place before I pick Sarah up. That enough time to make yourself all prettified?"

Aaron didn't answer. Instead, he pressed the power button on his phone, watching with a sense of sadness and finality as the screen went dark.

"What the hell are you doing?" Brian's face was glaring at him, the light from the TV throwing a smattering of dancing color onto his cheek.

Aaron winced and rubbed at his temple. "I—I just don't know if it's a good idea. If seeing him is a good idea."

Brian sighed. "I can't believe you're making me go through this again." He shook his head at Aaron's confused expression and picked up the remote, turning the volume down to almost nothing. "Unbelievable. You did the same thing when you started dating John, remember?"

It was hard to forget. John and Brian had been friends in high school, and when they ended up at the same college together, the two of them decided to make the most of it. They partied a lot harder than they had studied, but that all ended when Brian introduced John to his shy, recently outed roommate, and John decided it was love at first sight and would rather spend his nights wrapped in Aaron's arms, in Aaron's bed. Aaron hadn't been quite so sure. His experiences of relationships before college had ranged from bad to humiliating, and he couldn't quite get his head around the fact that someone like John would want someone like him. And poor Brian had ended up in the middle of it all.

"I'll say the same things I said then. You like this guy?" Brian sounded almost pissed off.

Aaron squirmed in his seat but in the end had to sigh and nod. "Yeah, I do."

"You like spending time with him?"

"Jesus, Bri."

"You wanna do all the gay lovin' nastiness with him?" Aaron huffed out a laugh and tried to hide his smirk. It didn't work. "Oh my God, you didn't already—y'know what, I don't want to know." Brian waved a dismissive hand at him and sat back in his chair.

They fell into a silent impasse, the voices of the announcers sounding tinny with the sound turned down so low, until Brian said softly, "You know what John would say."

Aaron nodded. "Yeah. Doesn't make it any easier. I feel like—like I'm being unfaithful to him. To his memory."

Brian was quiet. He rubbed his hand thoughtfully over his short beard, then sat up and leaned on the arm of his chair to look over. "I think part of the problem is that you're not remembering him right. You've got this picture in your head but it's not complete. It's like you're looking at him through grief-tinted glasses." Aaron slowly turned and glared at Brian but he didn't back down. "I was there, remember? Through all of it. All the arguing and bitching. Like when you kicked him out of the house for three days after he kissed Felix at your birthday party?"

Aaron scowled. "It wasn't three days."

Brian laughed bitterly. "It was. I know because he slept on my damn couch with his utter lack of remorse until I had to spell out to him just how upset you were. And what about all those unholy fights you used to have about money? Or the screaming matches about your family? How many times did you guys actually come to blows, huh?"

Aaron opened his mouth to deny it, a full flow of indignation and defensiveness rising in his throat, but it never came.

Brian raised his eyebrows and shook his head in that infuriating *I told you so* kind of way. "What you had together was great, but John wasn't a god, Ronny. He wasn't perfect. Neither are you, by the way, and I can almost guarantee this new guy isn't either. No one is saying you have to stop loving John to love this new guy. But you have to give him a chance. You have to give yourself a chance, and start living your fucking life again."

Aaron stared, the lump in his throat threatening to choke him. But he managed to swallow it down before tears welled in his eyes. "You get that from Hallmark?"

Brian grunted and settled back in his chair with a pinched, "Shut the fuck up and text the poor bastard back."

Aaron smiled sadly and huffed out a laugh as he turned his phone back on.

I love Alonzo's. See you at 7.

****

The sidewalk was packed so tight with last minute shoppers that Aaron wasn't sure he was going to make it to the restaurant by seven. The temperatures had dropped in the last week or so, which meant everybody was in thick winter coats that made their bulk double in size. Getting anywhere was like trying to navigate through a herd of Michelin men. There had been a flurry of snow or two but nothing had settled yet, much to Aaron's disappointment. Although he was relieved not to have to deal with icy streets on top of the foot traffic as he tried to elbow his way through Manhattan.

Still, it was hard to feel irritated, not with all the joyful lights and sparkling decorations reflecting off the wet streets, elaborate shop displays brightening up the place, Santas ringing bells on every other street corner behind the plumes of steam coming from below, and random people wishing him a Merry Christmas. And of course, the buzzing from his insides, knowing he was going to see Dylan again.

It had been weeks, and even though they messaged each other all the time, Aaron was surprised to find he actually missed Dylan. It was a strange feeling, to have a sense of hope—to loathe the absence of a person, but knowing it would come to an end eventually. He'd grown accustomed to grief. And as much as he felt guilty about letting it go, he really wanted to trust this new feeling would work out.

When he finally got to the restaurant—its usual red awning draped with festive greenery and the same sparkling lights that filled its windows—Aaron was brimming over with excitement as he pushed his way through the glass door. He looked around, figuring it shouldn't be too hard to spot Dylan's red hair amongst the patrons crowding into the place. Except he couldn't see him.

Aaron stood by the door, drawing his scarf from around his neck so he didn't overheat in the warm room, and peered around. The place was packed. There seemed to be a couple of large parties, raucously laughing and getting into the Christmas cheer, and most of the other tables and booths seemed to be occupied by couples and families, all smiling and laughing along with the festive music filling the air, alongside the aroma of home cooked Italian food.

A waitress started towards him, an anxious look on her face and a silver tray held against her chest, clearly about to turn him away, but just as she got to him, Aaron spotted a figure at the back of the room. He smiled at her before she even got to say anything and pointed toward Dylan. "I see my table. Thank you." The way he hurried away from her might have been considered rude but Aaron couldn't wait a moment longer. His nerves were getting the better of him.

He wasn't sure what he expected exactly, not declarations of love or any sort of huge emotional reunion. But a smile would have been nice or at the very least a hello. What he didn't expect was to find Dylan slumped down in the booth, holding his head in his hands looking more unhappy than Aaron thought he'd ever seen a person.

When Aaron slid into the seat next to him and gently touched his arm, Dylan jerked back and looked up at him with wide eyes, his complexion pale beneath the veneer of sun-kissed freckles. Dylan closed his eyes and whispered under his breath, "Shit."

Aaron sat back. "Wow. You want me to go?"

Dylan looked at him horrified, then reached out, desperately pulling him into his arms. "God, no! No. I'm so happy to see you, Clarence, I am. I just..." He buried his face in Aaron's neck and held him tight.

Aaron didn't let go despite the sense of dread that burned through him. "Christ, Dylan, are you okay? What's happened? Is it Kevin? Your mom?"

Dylan shook his head. He took a deep breath, still glued to Aaron's body but sat up when a peal of laughter came from one of the other tables. He glared over for a second then slumped down into his seat covering his face with his hands.

Aaron leaned over the table and looked over toward the crowd that seemed to be causing Dylan such consternation, and immediately understood why Dylan was freaking out.

He recognized Trey—the owner of the nightclub he and John used to frequent and Dylan's ex-boyfriend—immediately. He was hard to miss. Big and brash as always with his arm around some pretty kid who could have easily passed for seventeen. They were surrounded by people, all crowding over the table to try to get as close as possible, hoping to absorb some popularity by osmosis. Everyone was laughing and drinking and making a show of having a good time. And the twink was waving his left hand around.

Aaron slumped back in the seat. "Shit." He slid over to Dylan, pressing up against him so he could whisper, "What do you want to do? We don't have to stay here."

Dylan made a keening noise and pushed his hands up and through his hair, making it bounce every which way. "This is so fucked up. I'm so sorry. This was supposed to be...I'm so sorry."

Aaron didn't even think about where they were or who might be watching. He leaned forward and kissed Dylan on the mouth in lieu of declaring forgiveness. "Come on. Get your coat."

Aaron was acutely aware that they had to pass Trey's table in order to get out the door, so he made a plan of sorts as he pulled out his wallet and threw a couple of tens on the table. As soon as Dylan had his coat on, Aaron used his body as a shield, tucking Dylan in close to him with his arm around Dylan's shoulders, and made for the door.

They almost made it.

As Aaron pulled the door open, he heard a voice cry out from behind them. "Dylan? Is that you? Come and have a drink! We're celebrating!" He bundled Dylan out onto the street trying to ignore the cruel laughter that followed them out. Aaron kept tight hold of Dylan's arm as he practically launched himself in front of a taxi. When it screeched to a halt, he quickly bundled Dylan into the back and gave the driver an address where he knew they wouldn't be bothered.

Dylan didn't say a word in the cab. He even turned his back slightly to Aaron, hiding his face. Aaron tried not to take it personally. He figured bumping into your ex must be bad enough but being faced with your replacement...he couldn't imagine the emotions Dylan was going through.

Traffic was heavy but thankfully the cab driver took a route Aaron would never have thought of, that seemed to be slightly clearer. Aaron even learned a few new expletives, in what he was pretty sure was Turkish, by the time they reached their destination. Dylan stayed quiet and compliant when Aaron pulled him from the cab and pushed him towards the door of the bar.

It always amazed Aaron that no matter what time of year or what day of the week, Murphy's was always the same. Always the same five guys, sitting in the same five chairs, same music on the jukebox, and the same infuriating, flickering light over the pool table in the back. There might be the odd occasion when the place was overrun, on St Patrick's Day or during Fleet Week, but mostly the place was empty except for those five guys and a few other regulars who came and went. Aaron had decided early on it was probably a mob front but also that he didn't care. The beer was cold, and if you needed someplace to be where everyone left you the fuck alone, this was it.

He pushed Dylan ahead of him until they hit the bar. Dylan leaned on it with both elbows and covered his face. The bartender walked over with a quizzical look, drying a glass with a dishcloth. Aaron shook his head at him, willing him not to ask. Pulling off his scarf, Aaron nodded to the end of the bar. "Nice Christmas decorations." The small plastic tree with gaudy baubles and sad, threadbare tinsel looked like someone had pulled it from a dumpster.

The bartender nodded. "We thought we should make an effort this year." He pointed over at the plastic Santa looking cheekily over his shoulder sitting next to the cash register. When the button was pressed, a nasty sound started, like a Christmas carol being fed through a meat grinder, then Santa Ho-Ho-Hoed and pulled down his pants. Someone had drawn hairs all over his bare plastic ass with a Sharpie.

Aaron raised his eyebrows and nodded. "Very festive. Although you better be careful. Someone might mistake this place for Macy's."

The bartender snorted. "The usual?" Aaron held up two fingers and tipped his head towards Dylan, who hadn't moved. The bartender put two wide glasses on the table and poured the whiskey out. He paused; hand hovering as he looked with what could pass for concern at Aaron's companion. "You want me to leave the bottle?"

Aaron considered for a second, then shook his head. "Not yet. We'll ease into it."

Picking up the two glasses with the fingers of one hand, he put the other around Dylan's shoulders and steered him to a vacant table in a quiet corner. After shoving him into a chair and discarding his own coat, Aaron took hold of Dylan's fingers and wrapped them around one of the glasses. "Drink this."

Dylan looked dazed but did as he was told, tipping his head back and downing almost half the glass in one draft. His eyes bulged and he stared at Aaron for a second, then started coughing uncontrollably.

Aaron shook his head and patted him on the back, sounding completely unsympathetic when he said, "Jesus, I said drink it, not drown yourself in it."

Dylan wheezed in a breath. "What the hell is that?"

Aaron smiled gently at his own drink before he took a careful swig. He hissed and drew his lips back, baring his teeth. "Self-pity in a glass." Dylan cleared his throat. He picked up the glass again and sniffed at the dregs and recoiled. Aaron shook his head. "Take your medicine. It's good for you." Dylan grimaced but did as he was told, as Aaron finished his glass too.

Aaron sighed and sat back in his seat, watching Dylan finally come back to himself, shrugging off his coat as he unbuttoned it. He still looked shocked but at least had some color in his cheeks, looking less like he might pass out any minute. The bartender loped over out of nowhere and silently topped up their glasses. Clearly, Aaron had been a regular long enough that he warranted table service. Or maybe the bartender simply didn't want either of them cluttering up his bar.

"Thanks, Jimmy."

Aaron's smile wasn't returned. All he got from Jimmy was a curt, "Save it for the tip. And don't let him puke in here."

Aaron rolled his eyes as Jimmy walked away, watching the dishrag flapping from the back pocket of his jeans.

"You're going to tell me that he's a sweetheart underneath all that front, right?" Dylan's voice still sounded a little rough.

Aaron smiled softly. "Nope. Only time I've ever seen him smile is when he's talking about his kids."

Dylan scrubbed his hands over his face and leaned both elbows on the table. "I'm so sorry. I keep fucking this up, don't I?"

Aaron frowned at him. "You haven't fucked anything up." He sighed and wished he could wipe away all the turmoil that was clearly raging on Dylan's face. "You wanna talk about it?"

Dylan shook his head. "No." He took a sip of his whiskey and shuddered. But when the grimace left his face, the words started flowing. "That son of a... I just can't believe it y'know. Did you see? He's fucking marrying the guy. After three months! Two years we were together—Two years!—he wouldn't even give me the password to his Netflix account! I'm such an idiot—"

"Don't say that."

"No! I am! I really thought..." Dylan sighed, his whole body collapsing as he let out his breath. "I really thought he loved me. Despite everything. I really thought underneath it all that he needed me. It's the only reason I put up with all his shit—the only reason I defended him for all that time! I wasted two whole years of my life on that—"

Aaron couldn't stand the look on Dylan's face, the utter heartbreak of it all, so he reached out and pulled him in, holding him close, shushing him gently when his body shuddered. If there were angry sobs, the sound was muffled by the music from the jukebox.

When Aaron felt Dylan pull away, Aaron eased him out of his embrace, a little saddened by the loss. He touched his palm to Dylan's face as he sat back in the chair. "Maybe he did love you. Or maybe he didn't. What matters is that you were true to yourself."

Dylan huffed out a laugh. "You're so full of shit. What does that even mean?" He laughed again at Aaron's indignation and took his hand. "Mostly I feel stupid because I don't give two shits about Trey, but I'm still letting him ruin our evening." He smiled sadly. "I wanted to make tonight really special."

Aaron shrugged. "We can go to Alonzo's anytime."

"That's—that's not what I meant." Dylan sighed. "I missed you. This whole month, I've missed you and I really wanted to...I don't know."

Aaron smiled softly. "Romance me?"

Dylan blushed but smirked up at him. "Yes! I thought you might think it was...I don't know...if I dropped everything and came rushing back here to see you."

Aaron smiled softly down at his drink. He did think it was romantic. An amazing, wonderful, crazy gesture that made him feel really special. But all he said was, "I bet your mom wasn't happy about it."

Dylan smiled and shrugged. "Nope. But once Joe got through with her, she actually drove me to the airport and paid for half my ticket." Aaron laughed, but Dylan just sighed and frowned. "And then I go and ruin it freaking out over that...asshole." He sighed and ran his hand through his hair. "You must think I'm pathetic."

"Actually, all I can think is that I'm hungry. And you must be too. I know public displays of despair always wear me out." Aaron grinned at Dylan's half-hearted glare. "You like roast beef? Jimmy makes a mean roast beef sandwich. Bread so thick you can barely get it in your mouth. Just the right amount of horseradish."

Dylan frowned and looked around. "I don't see a menu."

"No menu. You just ask and food appears."

"Barely fits in your mouth, huh?"

Aaron didn't miss the smirk trying to stretch out Dylan's lips and he couldn't help wetting his own. "Well, I'm sure you'll have no problem as I recall..."

Aaron had to adjust himself as he walked to the bar. The two empty glasses he carried clinked together as he set them down.

"Same again," Jimmy asked as he wiped the counter.

"No. Can I get two of bottles of that IPA you pushed on me last week, and some sandwiches if the kitchen's open?"

Jimmy nodded. As Aaron settled on a bar stool to wait, he heard a mumbled, "Fucking faggots," from his right. He turned to see Charlie sitting there, a regular, just at that tipping point from old to decrepit. He looked like he might have been a boxer back in the day, or maybe an enforcer if Aaron stuck to his mob front fantasy. But now he was just an old man, with only a few teeth left in his head and even less hair underneath his ball cap. Charlie was one of the five regulars he thought might live here and pretty much always greeted Aaron the same way.

"Hi, Charlie. How's the missus?" Aaron had to grit his teeth to not react to the slur but still managed to sound friendly enough.

"None of your fucking business." Charlie took a slurp from his overfilled glass. Only the old timers were brave enough to drink anything on tap. "You still taking it up the ass?"

"Only on Sundays." Aaron took the two bottles that Jimmy put in front of him, along with an apologetic look. He slipped off the stool, saying with a sigh, "Y'know, maybe you should try it, Charlie. Might put a smile on that ugly mug of yours."

Charlie turned to look at him. A smile broke through his wrinkled chops, making him look less like an aging mobster for a moment and more like a grandpa. There was amusement but also a glint in his eye that made Aaron think that twenty years ago, Charlie would have cut him for saying such a thing and would have had no problem watching Aaron bleed out while he finished his beer. All the old man said was, "Well...maybe I will."

Aaron smirked. "Merry Christmas, Charlie."

Charlie raised his glass to him. "Merry Christmas, and same to your pansy friend too."

Dylan watched Aaron return to the table with a quizzical and slightly concerned expression on his face. "You have some interesting friends."

Aaron looked back over at the bar. "Who? Charlie? Oh, he's harmless enough." Dylan looked like he wasn't quite buying it. Aaron shrugged. "I started coming in here after John...It became a bit of a joke in the end, the drunken queer crying in the corner at noon on a weekday." He cleared his throat and shifted in his seat. "They got me through it."

Dylan's face fell and he looked down at the table. "I wish I could have been there for you."

Aaron shook his head. "No. I wouldn't have let you. Besides, you're here now, that's what counts."

They talked a little, drank and ate, and by the time they staggered out the front door into a flurry of snow, it still wasn't very late. They wandered the streets for a while, sometimes rubbing shoulders, occasionally holding hands if they thought they could get away with not being noticed. The way the light snowfall buzzed around them, illuminated in patches by the street lights made them feel like they were in their own little bubble.

They talked about Dylan's trip, his mom, and Florida, and how Aaron had spent the weeks alone; about anything but what had happened in the restaurant.

"I'm getting cold. Have you decided what you want to do?" Aaron pushed his hands deeper into his pockets. Dylan seemed to be undecided about whether he wanted to go home.

Dylan grinned over at him, his hair jeweled and sparkling with snow. "You."

Aaron huffed and shook his head, but he smiled and took Dylan's hand, turning in the direction of his apartment.

"Y'know, I haven't asked you about your plans for tomorrow." Dylan seemed a little reluctant to mention it.

"Going up to Brian and Sarah's for dinner. It's just going to be them and the kids—and Sarah's mother, who is probably the funniest woman I've ever met so it should be all right." He glanced over at Dylan who was watching his feet as they trudged along. "You're invited, by the way. If you don't already have plans, I mean." He tried to sound casual, like it was no big deal to ask. Except his heart started doing that jackrabbit thing as soon as the words left his lips.

Dylan looked truly surprised. "What?"

Aaron shrugged. "Brian suggested it. But if you made plans already—"

"No." Dylan huffed out a laugh. "No, this was a bit...spur of the moment."

Aaron smiled at him. "You didn't strike me as a spur of the moment kinda guy."

"I'm not. At all. Not normally. But something about you makes me want to take a chance." He glanced over at Aaron and slipped his icy hand into Aaron's pocket. "And I really wanted to see you."

Aaron didn't know what to say. He felt his cheeks get hot, despite the freezing air, and smiled into his scarf, taking Dylan's hand in his. "So, you'll come. To dinner."

They took the last few steps up to the front door of Aaron's apartment block. Dylan was quiet as Aaron dug the keys out of his pocket, but when Aaron paused before opening the door, he nodded and murmured, "Okay."

Aaron hung back a little when he let them into his apartment, partly out of nervousness but also to give Dylan some time to absorb the changes Aaron had made.

It looked a little different from the last time Dylan had been there. The walls were a warm gray now, not the stained magnolia from before. It made the whole place feel more homey. It had also helped when Aaron had put some pictures up on the wall, gifts from friends that he'd kept in a box in his closet. There was a new rug and bright cushions, even a few plants. It looked like a home finally. No more living out of boxes.

Dylan looked around, clearly amazed at the change, as he shook his coat from his shoulders. "I like what you've done with the place." Aaron shrugged like it was nothing. Dylan smiled. "You even have drapes."

Aaron huffed out a laugh. "Well, I thought after you called me out on what a mess it was, I should make an effort." Dylan looked apologetic but Aaron shushed him. "No really, you were the only person to point out I hadn't made any effort to really...I don't know...settle. You made me realize I wasn't living here so much as staying here. I figured it was time to move in. And maybe move on."

Dylan smiled softly. "In that case, you're welcome." They looked at each other for a moment, before Dylan's eyes darted over to the bedroom door. "So." He let the vowel linger. "Are all the changes just in here or...?"

Aaron tilted his head and shrugged. "Maybe you should take a look." He toed off his shoes and watched Dylan's smile widen as Dylan walked over to the door.

Dylan looked over his shoulder as he opened the door. "You coming?"

Aaron smirked and sighed out, "Oh, I sure hope so," and followed him in.

The room was repainted the same as the living room. The bed was made up with fresh dark blue bedding. Aaron tried not to admit to himself that the main reason he'd picked the color was so he could imagine Dylan's pale skin and red hair against it. Which he had—several times—in the intervening weeks.

Dylan stood at the foot of the bed, tracing his fingers over the fabric. He glanced up as Aaron came in.

"Nice," was all he said but he looked nervous for a moment, like he'd overstepped his boundaries.

Aaron walked straight up to him, pressing his chest against Dylan's; wanting to really feel his presence so he could know for sure this wasn't a dream. He lowered his head and kissed Dylan's neck, in the place under his ear that Aaron daydreamed about when he should be doing other things.

"Thanks," Aaron said, "I'm glad you like it."

Dylan shivered. "Fuck," he whispered, then brought his hands up, running them up the sides of Aaron's neck until they lodged in his hair. He pulled Aaron's mouth towards him and kissed him like a man possessed, taking any break in connection to murmur, "I missed you. Fuck, I really missed you."

Aaron felt giddy, lightheaded and high. He couldn't stop his hands from moving frantically over Dylan's back and shoulders, reaching down to cup his ass and knead his thighs, wanting to get closer even though he could feel his own erection rubbing blissfully against Dylan's. Aaron pushed back and started clawing at Dylan's shirt, saying breathlessly, "Naked. We should definitely be naked."

It didn't take them long. Aaron was pretty sure he lost a button, and nearly strangled himself trying to get his shirt over his head, but finally, he hopped over as he removed his sock and crawled onto the bed between Dylan's splayed legs.

Aaron settled his weight carefully onto Dylan, taking care to line his bobbing erection against Dylan's cock where it lay fat and full against his belly. Looking down, Aaron gently pushed Dylan's hair away from his eyes. "You look good in my bed."

Dylan's mouth fell open with a short gasp as Aaron rocked against him. He smirked. "Damn, I feel pretty good too."

Aaron rocked again and dropped his head to rest on Dylan's shoulder. "Fuck. You sure do."

They kept moving, the tendons on Aaron's forearms and neck straining even when Dylan arched up to meet him. Aaron kissed Dylan, licking inside his mouth and biting when the sensation became too much. Dylan moaned and Aaron couldn't hold back—didn't want to hold back. His fingers dug into Dylan's shoulders and he drove his hips forward as he came.

Aaron gasped for breath and tried to keep moving even though he was spent but Dylan keened with frustration and pushed Aaron back. Dylan took hold of his cock, pumping his hand frenetically, until his head fell back against the sheets and his hips pulsed upwards, as he sprayed over his chest.

Aaron leaned over Dylan, bending to kiss the perspiration from his throat, before collapsing on the bed next to him. They lay there side-by-side for a while, panting, waiting to recover. At some point, Aaron's fingers found Dylan's and they held hands. It felt like it was such an innocent gesture, which struck Aaron as funny given their current state, but also there was something about it that was almost more intimate than what they had just done together.

After a while, Aaron sat up and leaned across to grab the towel draped over the top of the laundry basket. He wiped himself down and made a fairly decent job of cleaning up the mess he'd made of Dylan, while Dylan just looked up at him, all freckles and pale skin and a soft, almost sad, smile.

"We should take a shower," Aaron said even though he was already lying back down.

Dylan rolled into him, snuggling close, resting his head on Aaron's shoulder and pulling the duvet with him to cover them. "No, don't leave. Let's just stay here a little while longer."

Aaron wanted to protest but his eyes were already drooping shut.

****

Aaron wasn't sure what woke him. It could have been a noise or glint of light through the curtains. He wasn't surprised to find he was alone until he realized for once, he shouldn't be. He reached out into the empty space beside him, running his hand over the sheet. It was cooling but not cold, and even in the darkened room he could see the scattered clothes Dylan had been wearing on their date. Unless Dylan had left in a panic and run naked into the street, Aaron felt satisfied he would come back to bed soon.

Except he didn't. Aaron lay there fully expecting Dylan to creep back under the covers at any moment, gradually changing from sleepy-headed to wide-awake and worried when it didn't happen. Eventually, Aaron couldn't wait any longer. He swung his legs over the side of the mattress, managed to find his boxers and undershirt, and went to look for Dylan.

It wasn't like Dylan would have had many places to hide, but Aaron pulled open the door, and saw Dylan immediately, standing at the large window looking out on the snow falling against the dark sky, illuminated by the street lights below.

Aaron didn't say anything but Dylan seemed to sense his presence, ducking his head and sighing as Aaron approached him.

"You okay?" Dylan didn't move or respond so Aaron took a step closer, asking quietly, "Can't sleep?"

Dylan sighed again, then turned to look at Aaron, his eyes pale enough with his skin to make him look ghostly. "What's going on between us, Clarence?"

Aaron was taken aback to hear the name again. He shrugged and folded his arms across his chest. "What do you mean?"

Dylan turned to face him, unashamedly naked. "I mean...is this going anywhere? Or am I just a distraction to you?"

Aaron scowled. "I don't...where is this coming from?"

Dylan ran his hand over his mouth and looked back out into the night. "You were talking to John in your sleep,"

Aaron closed his eyes and sighed. "Shit." He unfolded his arms and took a step toward Dylan, suddenly feeling guilty, and yet ridiculous at the same time for feeling that way about something he had no control over. "I didn't know I did that. Since I met you...I hardly dream about him anymore. But even if I did, he was my husband, Dylan. I loved him. I miss him."

Dylan winced and covered his eyes with his hand. "I know, I do. I know I'm asking too much...expecting you to feel the same about me."

"I don't." Aaron regretted the choice of words as soon as they left him and he reached out to Dylan even when he backed away. "I mean...I don't want what I had with John with you. I want something new, something that's just us. I don't know what that is yet. But I want to try, Dylan."

Dylan shook his head and swallowed hard. His voice was shaking when he finally spoke. "I—I need to tell you something. I have to confess." Aaron's heart sank, and it felt like his skin was shrinking too. He had to catch his breath when Dylan looked at him with a haunted expression on his face. "I really care about you.

If you want to try then I—I have to be honest with you. Even if it means you don't want to know me anymore."

"Jesus Christ, Dylan. You're scaring me."

"That night on the bridge—"

"Do I really need to know this—?"

"I didn't lie to you—"

"Dylan, stop—"

"That night on the bridge. I wasn't going to jump." Dylan opened his mouth but no words came out. He closed his eyes and tried again. "At least...I don't think I would have gone through with it."

"Oh, Dylan." Aaron took a step towards him, but Dylan pulled away, silhouetted against the windowpane.

"No. Don't. I—things are so different now, but then—that day, I couldn't see how it could ever get better. Trey made me believe no one could want me, that I was worthless and my life was pointless. That he was doing me a favor by being with me. I could never do anything right, I could never be right, for him or his friends. The only thing I had was him and then—" Dylan covered his face with his hands, his voice breaking under the strain, "Then even he didn't want me anymore, I didn't know what to do. I never really planned it or anything, but then I was there at the bridge and the thought just popped into my head."

Dylan pulled his hands away and looked at Aaron like he was his whole world. "And then suddenly you were there. Like a fucking angel out of nowhere." He sighed and shook his head. "I remember the morning after, writing that note to you, leaving my number, and all I could think about was about the text I wrote to my brother saying goodbye and how I'd been about a second away from sending it. And what that would have done to him." His eyes welled with tears. "I know you must hate me. I know I'm not good enough. I know—"

He didn't get to say anything else. Aaron enveloped him in his arms, crushing Dylan tightly to him, never wanting to let him go again. "I don't hate you. I could never hate you." Dylan protested, tried to pull away but Aaron held fast until he went still in Aaron's arms. Aaron kissed Dylan's hair and sighed. "We're flawed, you and I. But no one said we had to be perfect."

****

When Aaron woke for the second time, it could have been deja vu all over again when he felt the cold, empty space beside him but for the daylight coming through the curtains and the slamming of the front door.

Aaron sat bolt upright, hoping his worst fears weren't coming true. He and Dylan had talked a little more during the night, and they seemed to come to a decision to talk more on Christmas morning. Dylan seemed raw from the emotion of the day's events, and Aaron lay awake worrying for what seemed like hours about his fragile heart. It seemed those fears might have come true when he looked around to find Dylan's clothes and shoes no longer strewn about the place.

Aaron drew his knees up and buried his face his hands. He hadn't imagined that Dylan would run. He thought maybe Dylan might draw away from him, ghosting out of his life, embarrassed by his confession but Aaron at least thought they might have an adult conversation before Dylan was gone for good. But Dylan had seemed incredulous that Aaron could be so forgiving of him, that he had nothing but sympathy for the situation he had found himself in. It had made Aaron wonder, not for the first time, what hell he'd been through at the hands of Trey's manipulation to end up feeling that way. So maybe it was no surprise at all that he had disappeared.

Aaron was debating whether or not to throw on some clothes and try to go after him, when there was a muffled rustling noise from the living room. Aaron froze, thinking for one moment that it might be a burglar. But curiosity and common sense kicked in and he bounded out of bed, grabbing a hoodie from the rail as he passed it.

Of all the scenarios running through his head, the scene before him was not one of them. There was a Christmas tree in his living room. A real, modestly-sized tree complete with tinsel and baubles and some slightly-battered decorations, but a tree nonetheless. It rustled and swayed, then finally stilled, only for Dylan to pop up from behind it. He looked startled to see Aaron standing there, but then a huge smile cut across his face and he pointed at the tree with an out-stretched hand. "Merry

Christmas!" The tree started to topple, and Dylan had to grab it and adjust it, but then it seemed steady.

Aaron's eyebrows must have been in his hairline as he walked forward, his hands out in a gesture of disbelief. "Where in the hell did you get that?"

Dylan smirked and pulled the scarf from around his neck and started to unbutton his coat. "I have magical powers." Aaron tilted his head and glared, making Dylan laugh. "I wanted to get you breakfast, so I went to that bakery you said you liked. And then on the way back, it was just sitting on the sidewalk."

Aaron frowned at it. "Someone must be having a bad morning."

Dylan came to stand in front of him, lightly touching his arms. "I figured maybe it could make up a little for ruining Christmas last night."

Aaron smiled and shook his head. "You didn't ruin anything, you idiot." He drew Dylan's arms around his waist and threw his own over Dylan's shoulders. He held him tight before murmuring, "Unless you forgot the baked goods."

Dylan kissed him on the neck. "I would never do that to you."

Aaron smiled again, self-satisfied and happy. Then he remembered—he jerked away, looking into Dylan's surprised face. "I got you something."

He pulled away from Dylan's embrace, jogging into the bedroom with Dylan's forlorn voice following him. "What do you mean? Come back here already."

Aaron did come back, holding out a small silver box tied with red ribbon before him. Dylan just looked at it in confusion until Aaron sighed and forcibly shoved it into his hand. "Merry Christmas."

Dylan didn't say a word. He looked in bewilderment at the box, touching the ribbon gently with his fingers, then spun away, taking a seat on the couch. As Dylan yanked the ribbon off, Aaron settled himself next to him to watch, holding his breath as Dylan slid the top from the box and carefully pulled back the tissue paper. It wasn't expensive but Aaron couldn't resist it when he saw it in the store window. It was a Christmas ornament, a bell in the form of a small ceramic angel with little lace wings that sparkled.

Dylan carefully pulled it out of the box and held it up by the string coming out of its head. It tinkled prettily when he moved it. He smiled up at Aaron. "Somebody got their wings." He laughed. "You know this is just about the gayest thing anyone's ever gotten me."

Aaron shrugged and smiled. "You're welcome."

Dylan stood up and walked to the tree. He spent a second finding a spot to place it, then carefully attached the angel. He stood back to look at his handiwork before turning to look at Aaron with embarrassment. "I didn't get you anything."

Aaron smiled. "You got me a tree. And breakfast."

Dylan sighed and reached out to him. "I know, but I should have got you something. A gift."

Aaron stood and took his hand. "A year." Dylan looked confused but Aaron just smiled. "Give me a year."

Dylan frowned. "A year?"

Aaron nodded. "You asked me last night if this was going anywhere." Dylan started to protest but Aaron talked over him. "Since I met you, the question I keep asking myself is am I ready? And I have to say, I still don't know. Plus, I know Kevin is worried you've just imprinted on me like a baby duck or something—"

"He said that?" Dylan looked mortified.

"Not in so many words. But he said that you've been through a lot with Trey, and after last night, I'm even more certain you're not ready for another serious relationship either." Dylan started to breathe heavily and looked like he might run, so Aaron stepped forward and grabbed him by the biceps. "So, let's take a year, to get to know each other, to figure ourselves out. I like you. I want to be around you. So much. But I don't want to hurt you by promising something we both might later regret."

Dylan nodded, looking seriously at the floor. Eventually, he sighed and raised his head. "A year, huh?" Aaron nodded. "A lot can happen in a year, Clarence."

Aaron smiled. "You willing to find out just how much?"

Dylan kissed him. "Like I said, you make me want to take a chance. And I can't think of a single reason to say no to you."

Epilogue

The wind had died down from the night before, and Aaron was grateful. The weather had turned icy cold in November and for a while it seemed like the snow would never stop. Not that Aaron would complain about it, but walking up to the top of the hill on a freezing Christmas morning, he was glad for the blue sky, and the few swirling flakes in the air.

The roads had been cleared, as had the driveways in the cemetery, but the usually well-kempt, luscious green grass was hidden beneath snow deep enough to cover his boots and dampen the bottom of his jeans as he trudged through it. The gravestones had been blasted by the previous night's storm, leaving them caked in snow from this angle, although the winter sun had started to thaw it, smoothing out the rough patches and melting the surface that would freeze later in a crisp layer of ice. Most of the names had been obliterated but Aaron didn't need to see them to know where he was going. He'd been coming here almost two years. He knew the route by heart.

Coming to stand in front of the headstone, Aaron sighed as he squatted down and brushed the snow from the granite face, running the tip of his gloved finger through the gouges that spelled out John's name.

"Hey, Baby." Aaron knew he didn't need to say the words aloud, but it always felt good to come here and talk. "Merry Christmas."

Aaron felt a lump form in his throat but swallowed it down. He didn't want to be sad anymore. He'd actually said those very words to his therapist six months before. They'd talked it over during their session—she'd done a good job of containing her excitement at his breakthrough—then Aaron had gone straight to meet Dylan at work and asked him to move in. Of course, Dylan had said no. But he softened his objection by making out that Aaron's place was too small. But when Aaron's lease was up, they'd gone ahead and found a new place, somewhere they could make new memories together. Somewhere they could both make a fresh start.

Aaron had been loathe to wait but in the end, it turned out fine. They managed to get a place closer to Aaron's school, which meant almost no commuting time, something that made a big difference since Dylan had started taking night classes. For a while they had been ships in the night, only seeing each other at weekends when they would inevitably fall asleep on the couch under textbooks that needed reading and term papers that needed marking.

But even after they started living together it hadn't been plain sailing. There were small things; like Aaron's inability to make a decision about the simplest thing. There seemed to be a limit on how many times Dylan was willing to take, "I don't mind, you decide," as an answer before blowing his top. Aaron hadn't realized how he had become so used to John making the simplest of decisions for him. It was somewhat of a revelation to find out he actually preferred poached eggs, not fried, and that he liked rom-coms better than action movies.

And then there came the big adjustments; like Aaron assuming that Dylan was OCD when it came to the cleaning and cooking. The first few weeks they lived together, Aaron didn't have to lift a finger, even when he kept offering to help. But coming home early from work one day, looking forward to spending some quality time with Dylan before he left for his shift, Aaron realized it was something else altogether.

Dylan had blanched when Aaron walked through the door. He'd looked terrified and started immediately straightening the couch, and trying to clear away his things, all the while apologizing, almost on the verge of tears. Aaron had ended up having to physically stop him, holding him tight in his arms and teasing the truth out of him. It took some convincing that Aaron didn't want Dylan to cook or clean or keep any of the unreasonable expectations or rules that Trey had forced on him. And when it became clear that Dylan was struggling to let that stuff go, Aaron had dragged him to couple's therapy to see if that would help and then Dylan saw a therapist on his own for a while. The first time Dylan had left the dishes in the sink after dinner and joined Aaron on the couch, it felt like such a victory, even though Dylan's palms were sweating when Aaron took his hand.

At times, their developing relationship had felt like a battle, not with each other but with their own lingering issues. But standing at John's graveside, Aaron thought they had finally won.

Aaron cleared his throat. "I wasn't sure whether to come today." He reached out and placed his gloved hand on the cold stone. "But I have something to tell you." He swallowed again and closed his eyes. The air was cold but he felt the warmth of the sun breaking through and couldn't help but smile.

"Dylan asked me to marry him. I told him I needed to talk it over with you." A gust of wind whipped by and Aaron dropped his hand and stood slowly. He shoved his hands in his pockets and looked down at the frozen ground. "I think I'm going to say yes. Mostly because he doesn't laugh at me when I say shit like that. And when I miss you, he just holds me and we talk about the good times you and I had. I don't know anyone else who would do that."

Aaron pressed his lips together and shuffled his feet, watching the snow pack down under his boots. "Anyway. I didn't want to say yes until I'd talked to you about it. I think Dylan knows already, but it didn't seem right until I'd told you first. I'm sure Kev will have lots to say about closure...he does like talking about all that psychological stuff. I suppose we'll tell Brian and Sarah later..." Aaron sighed and looked around at the blue sky, barren trees and view over the river and the city, and thought how beautiful the place was. "So, if you have any objections, y'know, a bolt of lightning or dead bird falling from the sky type omen, now's the time to do it."

Aaron held his breath, feeling a little stupid about saying it but more so about the real sense of dread that came over him, as if something might actually happen. After a minute where the wind seemed to still and he could only hear the faint sounds of traffic in the distance and a bell ringing somewhere, he let out the breath he'd been holding. "Okay then. I guess I have your blessing." He smiled. "I am glad...'cause I love him, John. He makes me happy and I really do love him."

Aaron stood in silence for a moment longer. He turned to leave, but stopped and turned back, pulling a small crumpled package from his pocket. Crouching back down, he brushed the snow from the foot of the headstone and gently propped the box against it. The thin Christmas paper immediately started to darken where it touched the snow but it didn't matter. Aaron leaned forward resting his forehead on the cold stone for a moment, then stood and turned, walking away without a word.

Dylan was waiting for him at the car. He stood, leaning back against the hood, his hands stuffed deep into the pockets of his long coat, his shoulders bunched up around his ears. He'd grown a beard this last fall, thick and red. He pretended to hate it when Aaron started calling him Pumpkin Spice Santa, but Dylan hadn't stopped him. Aaron shook his head as he walked the last few steps through the snow. "Why didn't you wait in the car?"

Dylan shrugged. "I never wait in the car." He held out his arms, just like he always did and Aaron fell into them. He lay against Dylan's body for a moment, allowing himself the comfort as Dylan put his arms around him and kissed his hair. Aaron's ritual of visiting John graveside had become *their* ritual somewhere along the way.

"So," Dylan asked, "What did he say?" He did a really bad job of covering up his impatience at the best of times.

Aaron shrugged without attempting to move from Dylan's embrace. "He said he has to think about it." Dylan's sighed with overly dramatic exasperation and Aaron couldn't help but laugh. He liked that; that he and Dylan had come finally to a place in their relationship where they could tease and laugh. For a while there, the serious conversations and heartfelt negotiations for intimacy and trust out-weighed the fun moments considerably. But little by little, they started to laugh more and more, until now Aaron felt like he had the capacity to smile all day long. And that Dylan had made that possible. "He didn't say anything. Did you really think he would?"

Dylan held him tighter. "If he had, I'd be driving you straight to your therapist, Christmas morning be damned."

Aaron sighed. "Will it still be all right to come here, if I need to? After we're married?"

He felt Dylan smile against his cheek. "Of course."

"Joe's going to be unbearable with the wedding arrangements, isn't he?"

Dylan nodded. "Yes, he is. But then, he is a romantic."

Aaron huffed out a laugh and pulled back to look into the gray eyes he loved so much, unsurprised to find them wet with tears. "And you're not?"

Dylan shrugged. "Whatever. Merry Christmas, Clarence."

Aaron smiled and kissed him. "And a Happy New Year to you, George."

The End

Thank You For Reading

Thank you for reading *'Tis the Season*. I hope you enjoyed it.
If you'd like to leave a review on Goodreads, Amazon or anywhere else, that would be very much appreciated.
If you like to get in touch, I'd love to hear from you.
If you'd like to hear from me, I have a newsletter—you can sign up on my website.

If you're affected by any of the themes in this story, please don't feel that you are alone. If you need to talk to someone and don't feel like speaking to friends, family or your doctor, don't be afraid to contact your local helpline services. You should be able to find one in your area through this website. www.suicideprevention.wikia.com

About the Author

After spending far too long creating stories in her head, Alex finally plucked up the courage to write them down and realized it was quite fun seeing them on the page after all.

Free from aspirations of literary greatness, Alex simply hopes to entertain by spinning a good yarn of love and life, wrapped up with a happy ending. Although, if her characters have to go through Hell to get there, she's a-okay with that.

With only a dysfunctional taste in music and a one-eyed dog to otherwise fill her days, Alex writes and walks on the South Coast of England—even when her heart and spellcheck are in New York.

www.alexjane.info
contact@alexjane.info

Also by the Author

The Alphas' Homestead Series

#1 - Home Is Where You Are
#2 - Returning Home
#3 – Longing for Shelter

The Mr and Mr Detective Stories

#1 – Gazes Into You

The Alphas' Homestead Series - Book One

Home Is Where You Are

By the winter of 1870, Caleb Fletcher has carved out a sheltered existence for himself in a simple cabin, outside a small town in the backwaters of Nebraska, resigned to living out his days as a solitary wolf. But his quiet life is interrupted when another werewolf lands on his doorstep on the eve of a snowstorm, brutalized almost beyond repair, with nowhere else to turn.

When Caleb reluctantly welcomes Jacob into his cabin, and eventually his bed, it forces him to face up to the traumas he's been running from; the shame that made him leave his pack behind, and the horrors of war he endured.

As the weeks pass, it seems that Jacob's arrival might not be the coincidence it first appeared. Jacob has an agenda. One that involves Caleb. And if Caleb agrees to it – if he can let go of his past and his prejudices – it will change Caleb's whole world. Maybe even for the better.

Without a mate – a family, a pack – a wolf has no home.

But what if home finds you?

A Mr and Mr Detective Story - #1

Gazes Into You

Ex-detective John Right likes to watch.

There's no harm in it.

The latest object of his obsession—a twenty-something stranger who chains his bike outside John's office—doesn't feel the weight of John's eyes on him, doesn't know about the secret recordings or what John does with them in the dead of night. Except when the kid disappears, John finds himself doing far more that just watching.

Reluctantly, John has to start thinking like a cop once more as he frantically tries to track down his mystery man. Although when he finds him, John is left with more questions than answers. And the more he learns, the more he wishes he'd never started looking in the first place.

Can John get to the bottom of the mystery without giving away his own dirty secret? And without giving in to his urge to do more than simply watch?

Well…nobody's perfect.